CODE OF SILENCE

A NOVELLA BASED ON
CHARACTERS FROM NEXT TO DIE

MARLISS MELTON

JAMES-YORK PRESS

©James-York Press, P. O. Box 141, Williamsburg, VA23187

Published by James-York Press
Feb 2014/eBook
March 2014/paperback

Edited by Wendie Grogan and Sydney Baily-Gould
Book Cover Designed by: Wicked Smart Designs
Interior Pages Illustrated by: James-York Press
Interior Design by: BB ebooks

CHAPTER ONE

OPHELIA PRICE STARED in disbelief at the plus sign on the plastic pregnancy test strip. *Oh, my God.* She could not have been more astounded if the bathroom ceiling suddenly collapsed on top of her head. She'd taken this same test twice before in the past ten years, and they'd both shown up negative. That plus sign was not supposed to be there, not when she'd taken the pill more or less regularly for over a decade and her periods had come like clockwork, at least until this month. With her period three weeks late, she'd decided to take the test, but only as a precautionary measure, never dreaming that the results would be what they were.

It had to be a mistake. Only it said right there on the box: 98% accurate. And she had been feeling a teeny bit sick every morning for the past two weeks.

I'm pregnant.

Her heart beat a tattoo of denial. An icy numbness filled her heart. The timing could not be worse.

In the past five years, her job in journalism had taken off, elevating her to the position of lead investigative reporter. WTKR had stolen her away from WAVY television by offering her an obscene salary to go after every dirty cop, corporation, or politician she could find. For a girl who'd once wasted her degree in journalism by waitressing at Hooters, she'd sure come a long way. And she owed a lot of her success—most of it, in fact—to her new husband, Vinny, and his faith in her. Now she made the big bucks exposing fraud and corruption, and she loved what she did for a living.

I can't have a baby.

It would ruin everything. The fabulous run on her career would come to a screeching halt the moment she shared her news with anyone. Vinny, she had no doubt, would use her pregnancy as a reason for her to spend more time at home. And then there was her boss who would pull her off the set the minute she started showing—pregnant news reporters weren't sexy. Maternity leave would be the final nail in her coffin. She'd be relegated to small-time reporting—no more national scandals or multi-corporate shakedowns. And then who would she be? Just a mother, a job she was totally unfit for.

The light knock on the door startled the tester out of Ophelia's hand. It clattered to the tiled floor, skidding toward the toilet.

"You okay in there, *cara mia*?" Vinny asked with concern in his deep voice.

Locks had never been a deterrent to her husband. Snatching up the evidence lest he catch sight of it, Ophelia offered up a lie. "Just doing my makeup, hon. I'll be out in a sec."

She and Vinny had eloped while on vacation in Bermuda the previous spring. The spur-of-the-moment ceremony performed under a moon gate was just one more reason why his mother had come to resent her. It had taken Ophelia five years to marry her son, and then she'd gone and done it without his mother there to bear witness.

At times Ophelia regretted not having shared that special moment the way they should have, with Vinny's family and his fellow Navy SEALs present, along with her older sister Penny. But it had felt so right, so romantic, pledging her future to Vinny under the round stone arch overlooking the tourmaline sea. Besides, who had time to plan an elaborate wedding?

Vinny was her soul mate. She'd belonged to him even before she'd been ready to admit it. He knew her better than anyone. He also knew she was lying right then because she always put on her makeup in the car. He had to be rolling his eyes at her lame attempt to deceive him.

"Listen," he said, making her hold her breath, "how about we go to Mama's for Thanksgiving instead of her coming down this year? She says her washing machine doesn't work, and she needs me to fix it. Plus, I'm worried about her health."

He wanted to go to Philly for Thanksgiving? A spurt of excitement replaced her shock and self-doubt. Wait, could Vinny have guessed her plans to interview the lieutenant governor of Pennsylvania next month? No way. He wouldn't want them going anywhere near Philly if he had an inkling of what she intended.

"Ah, sure," she said, swinging a thoughtful look at her reflection in the mirror. "That sounds okay." She wasn't going to tell him either, or he'd change his mind about visiting his mother.

"Did you just say okay?" he responded, sounding incredulous. "I said, we need to go to Mama's for Thanksgiving," he repeated, enunciating each word.

"Yeah, why not?" Ophelia took one last look at the tester before stuffing it inside the tampon box under the sink.

A subtle click of the lock had her slamming the cabinet shut and straightening guiltily as the door swung slowly open. There stood Vinny peering around the door, his chocolate brown eyes locking on her guilty expression.

"I've told you not to do that!" Ophelia scolded. "A woman needs her privacy."

"I could tell you weren't on the toilet. What's going on?" he demanded.

She rolled her eyes. "Why do you think something's going on?"

He just looked at her in that intent, all-seeing way of his that made her toes curl inside of her high heeled shoes. "You just agreed to Thanksgiving at my mother's," he pointed out.

She strove for an innocent look. "Yes, I did."

Vinny's eyes narrowed, conveying utter skepticism. Ophelia never could resist those eyes. Rimmed with lush lashes, they sloped just enough that, combined with his hooked nose, they made him resemble a young Al Pacino. "Then you've forgiven her for her remark about your skinny hips?"

Ophelia forced a negligent shrug even though the reminder reawakened her resentment. "What's to forgive? She was upset that she'd missed our wedding. It's only natural that she would lash out about it. Any mother would be upset about missing her only son's wedding."

"True." Vinny nodded, his gaze still watchful. "But she said some pretty hurtful things," he acknowledged.

Rose's exact words had been that it was time she quit her job, put some meat on her skinny hips, and start being the wife that Vinny deserved. "She wants grandbabies," Ophelia reminded him with just a stitch of resentment left. "Who can blame her?" Guilt pinched her anew as she considered that she could now make Rose's dreams come true. But she had no intention of sharing that happy news—not yet, anyway.

Vinny's gentle smile did nothing to ease her conscience as he waded deeper into the bathroom, his arms outstretched. "Yeah, maybe we can work on that before you go to work this morning," he suggested in a husky voice, pulling her into his embrace. The musky sweat that clung to his T-shirt from his morning run prompted Ophelia to squirm free.

"You're going to soil my work clothes," she protested.

"Just a kiss then," he pleaded, catching her jaw in his hand and turning her head toward his. One touch of his warm, supple lips and Ophelia forgot about escaping.

Goosebumps played tag along her skin as his clever tongue coaxed her lips to part so he could offer her a glimpse of what she'd be missing. By the time he lifted his head, the floor seemed to be tilting and she was seriously considering getting undressed to join him in the shower. She grabbed his wrist to read his watch. "Oh, shoot, I'm late."

"You're always late," he pointed out. "What's another half hour?"

"No, seriously, I have to go. My new boss is making us sign in."

"The prick," Vinny exclaimed.

"Tell me about it." On the verge of slipping under his arm and out of the room, Ophelia pressed a heartfelt kiss on Vinny's cheek. "I love you," she told him, surprised to feel tears sting her eyes.

His dark eyebrows quirked. "I love you, too," he said.

She fled before he could question her. Vinny knew her like nobody else did, even better than her sister. If he guessed her circumstances, if he knew that their child was growing in her womb, he would move heaven and earth to get her to quit her job and stay at home, where their baby would be safe.

Over my dead body, Ophelia thought, exiting the bathroom swiftly and collecting her purse and jacket from the hall closet. Being the lead investigative reporter was the one thing she did well. It gave her the self-respect she desperately craved. Before her career in journalism, she'd been living with her sister because she couldn't support herself waitressing and indulging in pastimes that were self-destructive.

And then Vinny De Innocentis had come along. He might have been four years her junior, but he was so totally with-it, with a sound work-ethic, a career in the Navy, and a long-term goal of becoming a doctor. He'd inspired her to improve herself. Finally, she felt like she was worthy of him, but only because of her job.

If and when he found out she was pregnant, that would change—not just because Vinny would insist that she alter her priorities but also because being pregnant would ruin her career.

Maybe she wouldn't tell Vinny. The thought sneaked into her brain as she backed out of their single-car garage, executing a U-turn next to Vinny's Honda Civic. She could visit a clinic somewhere and quietly abort—*oh, God, no.* She dismissed the notion the instant it occurred to her. She could never do that to Vinny or their baby. Not when she already knew what a terrific father he would make. Not when he let her park her car in their one-car garage so she didn't have to run in and out of the weather. He deserved way better than that. He deserved better than *her.*

I'm a shitty person. Shame for having even considered an abortion made her swallow hard as she tugged the gear shift into drive and took off down Shore Drive in Virginia Beach, headed for Norfolk. But the fact remained that there were even shittier people out there pulling the wool over other people's eyes, manipulating the system in their endless quest for power. And if Ophelia Price didn't call those people onto the carpet to account for their sins, then who would?

Fixing her eyes on the road, she grubbed in her purse in search of the bronzer she usually applied as she drove. Vinny's chiding voice sounded in her head, arresting her search. *Baby, you don't need to do that. You're beautiful just the way you are.*

Pulling down the visor to look in the mirror there, she studied her reflection critically. Through her turquoise eyes, she admired her smart gray jacket and cream silk top. Back when Vinny had first met her she'd dressed like a hippy, not a professional. Her red-gold hair was pinned up in a loose but elegant knot. She leaned closer to the mirror, spying fine lines around her eyes and across her forehead. Did Vinny, who was all of twenty-five years old now, find her too mature? She would turn thirty in August.

Shutting the visor with a snap, she passed up the bronzer in favor of colored lip-gloss and decided to forego makeup otherwise. If she went on the air later, a makeup artist would put a ton of products on her then. She might be an inherently selfish person, but she didn't need to risk the secret life inside her for no reason whatsoever.

VINNY'S MOTHER STILL lived in the Italian neighborhood of Bella Vista in the same brick row house squeezed between two others just like it, on a street jammed with cars and sprinkled with debris. Whenever Ophelia took in his old stomping ground, she couldn't help but marvel at what he'd overcome.

"You're a saint," she decided of her husband as he parallel-parked her somewhat new, sunburnt orange Kia Soul between two beaters.

He issued a startled laugh. "Hardly." He slanted her a funny look. "What makes you say that?"

She just shook her head at his humility. Not only had Vinny resisted recruitment by the local gangs while growing up here, but he'd also helped to raise his little sister when their father ran off and his mother fell ill. "Most people are victims of their circumstances," she said with a grimace. "But you always take the high road." Which was probably why she felt like such a loser in comparison.

His purely Italian shrug sloughed off her praise. "Nah, it's a choice," he stated. "Everybody has a choice."

His words echoed in her head as he set the parking brake and punched the button that killed her engine. A frown of worry furrowed his forehead as he took in his former neighborhood. "We should'a brought my car. Someone's gonna key your car for bein' so new."

"Well, that's why I hit Penny's mailbox. Now the dent in the fender makes it look like all the other cars."

He chuckled and shook his head. "Oh, that's why you ran into the mailbox."

"Yep." Truth was, she thought she might just need her car to keep her appointment with the lieutenant governor, and she hadn't learned to drive Vinny's stick shift—or rather, he didn't trust her to drive his stick shift.

"And here I thought you wanted your car so you could leave if Mama hurt your feelings," he replied.

"That, too."

Vinny squeezed her hand. "She'll behave herself, I promise. Besides, Bella's here to distract her." He gestured toward his little sister's lime green Escort as he pushed out of the driver's seat. Ophelia followed suit, rounding the back of the car to help with their luggage. Isabella, now a student at Drexel University, was home for the holiday.

A chilly breeze redolent with the smells of garlic wafted from a nearby restaurant. As they climbed the home's front stoop, the door popped open. There stood Mama Rose, her doughy arms outstretched to greet them.

"*Figlio mio*," she exclaimed, drawing Vinny against her apron-clad bosom as he stepped up to greet her. If his shoulders weren't as wide as the door itself, the embrace might have swallowed him whole. "Welcome, welcome," she crooned. Kissing him soundly on both cheeks, she then regarded Ophelia through eyes identical to Vinny's. The thread of tension between them snapped as she shoved Vinny aside to embrace Ophelia with equal warmth. "Thank you for coming. I cook all day!" she exclaimed, her English as elementary as it had been since Ophelia first met her five years ago. "Come in, come! S'cold outside."

They hadn't moved beyond the foyer before the old staircase shuddered and Isabella DeInnocentis, as dark-haired and athletic as her brother, blew down from the upper level, colliding into Vinny at a full run. But he was ready for her, swinging her around to keep from staggering backwards. "Hey, sis! How's it goin'?"

"Better now that you're home," she said breathlessly.

He frowned at her, then looked at his mother. "What do you mean? What's wrong?"

"Nothing," his sister said airily. "I've just missed you, that's all."

"Humph." Their mother pursed her lips into a disapproving knot. "Your sister has a boyfriend," she said on a note of disgust.

"Mama!" Isabella rounded on her. "I told you not to tell."

"*Boyfriend*," Vinny repeated, scowling harder. "What the hell do you need a boyfriend for? You're a student. It's your job to study, not waste your time on some schmuck."

"Vinny!" Ophelia elbowed her way forward and threw an arm around her sister-in-law in a show of solidarity. "You can't tell her when she can or cannot fall in love." She turned her head to look at Isabella. "Who's the lucky guy?"

"His name is Robert and he's a philosophy major."

"Philosophy, hah." Vinny rolled his eyes. "What's he gonna do with that degree?"

Bella arched her eyebrows at him. "Go to law school," she said coolly.

"Oh." And suddenly Vinny had no more to say on the subject.

"Enough talk," Mama Rose declared. "Take your suitcase up and come to the kitchen for food."

"We just had subs on the way up, Mama," Vinny protested, hefting their shared suitcase and climbing the stairs to his old bedroom. Last Easter was the first time his mother had even let them share a bed. Considering they were *finally* married—even though *she* hadn't been invited—she hadn't had much choice.

Trailing Vinny into the tiny front room, Ophelia deposited her purse and cosmetics bag. She hadn't dared to bring her laptop or Vinny would have guessed that she was working on a story. She didn't need her laptop in any case. All the facts of the case were tucked away in her head. If Vinny had the slightest notion that she was on a deep-sea fishing expedition, angling for a really big prize, he'd have refused his mother's invitation to Philly and swept her off to some remote island somewhere.

TWO HOURS LATER, they sat in the narrow kitchen with the sky growing dark outside and Mama Rose stuffing an eight-pound turkey in preparation for tomorrow's feast. Listening to Bella regale them with stories of campus life, Ophelia waited for the opportunity to finagle time away from Vinny the next morning. She estimated that she would need at least two hours to get downtown, conduct her interview with Lieutenant Governor Rawlings, and get back to the house.

"Let's watch the Thanksgiving parade tomorrow," she suggested when Bella's stories came to an end. The parade was the only good excuse she could think of; unfortunately, it meant involving Bella in her plans. "You know it's the oldest ongoing parade in the country, right? I've never seen it."

Vinny shot her a considering look. "I'm gonna fix Mama's washing machine," he reminded her. They'd discussed it on the way up. He needed time alone with Mama to prod her about her health. She'd been complaining of fatigue and, having battled cancer a decade earlier, he wanted to find out what the doctors were saying.

"Bella and I can go by ourselves. No biggie," she assured him.

"Yeah, but a parade," he said reminding her that he deplored large gatherings for the fact that terrorists loved them. "Why don't you just go to a movie or something?"

"On Thanksgiving morning? The theaters aren't even open. Besides, a parade will get us in the holiday spirit with the floats, and the drums, and the bands. I can't wait!"

"Fine," Vinny conceded. "Just don't stand by any trash cans or planters."

Regretting the need to mislead him, she patted his hand consolingly. As much as she hated keeping secrets from her husband, what he didn't know couldn't hurt him. He was too protective, too prone to imagine bad things happening to her. This way, she'd conduct her interview and he'd never have to worry.

Later, when she managed to expose Jay Rawlings for the liar that he was, Vinny would realize what she'd done and when she'd done it, only by then it would be too late.

Better to ask forgiveness than permission. That'd been Ophelia's motto all of her life, and she didn't see any reason to change things up at this late date.

VINNY STRETCHED OUT on the length of his child-hood bed, his toes hitting the footboard. The double bed felt tiny compared to the king-sized monstrosity they had at home, but he positively loved the coziness of having Ophelia snuggled up against him. Now that they were married, his mother had *finally* relented and let them share a bed. No more having to sneak Ophelia in after midnight and then get her back into Bella's room by dawn. "This is so nice," he purred, sliding his hand up under his wife's night-shirt and down inside of her panties.

To his confusion, she seemed to stiffen slightly. What was that about? He backed off, smoothing the hourglass outline of her body from her hip to her shoulder. "You doin' okay, Lia?" he asked calling her by her nickname. Maybe his mama had made some comment that he hadn't overheard and Lia was gnawing on it, hurting on the inside.

"Yeah, sure," she said with forced brightness.

He turned his head, seeking her turquoise eyes in the dark. There they were, lit by the glow of the city and the beams of the street lamp slicing through the cracks in the curtains. "My mother didn't say some-thin' to hurt your feelings, did she?"

"No, not at all. I'm just thinking about the parade tomorrow, looking forward to it."

"Yeah? Ready to gorge yourself and put some meat on those skinny hips?" he quipped.

The sound she made in her throat told him that his joke sucked.

Besides, her hips weren't skinny. They were smooth and curvy, and the cool globe of her ass cheek filled his palm to perfection. He fitted his pelvis to hers as he kneaded her backside, letting her feel her effect on him. "You're perfect just the way you are," he rasped, sliding his hand up the delicate vertebrae of her spine and rejoicing inwardly as she arched and relaxed into his embrace.

She needed warming up was all. He knew how to do that. Matter of fact, getting Lia all hot and bothered was pretty much what he lived for ever since the day he dragged her to the top of the old lighthouse at Cape Henry. Remembering her astonishment when he'd made her come twice in mere minutes, he applied himself to the challenge of doing it again.

Lia's hum of pleasure was all the encouragement he needed to toss back the covers, strip off her drawers and replace his hand with his mouth. He nibbled his way to the juncture of her thighs, licking and nipping until she sighed in surrender and spread her legs in a silent plea. Sneaking a peek up the length of her luminous body, he was rewarded by the vision of her nightshirt pulled to her shoulders and her own hands on her breasts. Now *that* was sexy. He loved her taste, her scent, and her responsiveness. Not a day went by that he didn't thank God she was his.

Sure, she could be a handful. Sure, she got herself regularly into trouble by butting heads with people in positions of authority and upending the status quo. But, with Lia, there was never a dull moment.

His confidence grew as her skin grew heated. She trembled with excitement under his dancing tongue, her breath coming faster. He backed off intentionally, stoking the embers of her desire by degrees until he finally gave her what she wanted.

He knew the exact moment that her orgasm seized her, and he could only pray that she would stifle her cry of pleasure so his mama and sister couldn't overhear. She did, biting her lower lip as she rode the storm, then stretching languorously beneath him as he covered her body with his and filled her to the hilt.

Ah, yes. This was home. In her snug, silken warmth, he found his refuge, a place where he could return again and again to encounter bone-deep satisfaction. Wrapping her slim thighs around him, Lia pulled him closer, sought his mouth, and kissed him until he floated in a sea of sensation, their limbs entwined, their bodies merging.

"I love you so much, Vinny," she confessed between kisses.

She'd been saying that a lot lately. And while he could never hear it enough, the words were beginning to take on a portentous quality. She couldn't know if something bad was going to happen to either of them, could she? Nah, it was just his paranoid mind playing tricks on him. He pushed the unpleasant thought to the periphery and concentrated on the bliss that was taking his body by storm.

Oh, yeah. Oh, baby. It was like this every time—just too damn good to make holding off a viable option. He let ecstasy geyser through him. Groaning his surcease against her sweet-smelling neck, he acknowledged that he was the luckiest man alive, and nothing was going to change that fact anytime soon, not if he could help it.

"I love you, too, *cara mia.* Christ, I love you," he murmured into her ear. And then he promptly fell asleep.

CHAPTER TWO

OPHELIA RUBBED HER hands together briskly, wishing she'd thought to bring gloves. The beat of a bass drum filled her ears, overlaid by the blare of trumpets as a marching band tramped closer. She and Bella had arrived late and still managed to insinuate themselves among the crowd. They stood on the steps of the Philadelphia Art Museum, right where the parade ended. As float after float passed them, each one more colorful than the last, Ophelia's excitement about the upcoming holiday rose. Christmas motifs abounded, lifting her spirits. *I'll tell Vinny about the baby at Christmas,* she decided. Wouldn't that make a nice present!

Now she had a good reason for keeping her secret.

When at last the city council float came into view, marking the end of the parade and decorated with a massive Christmas tree that spired twenty feet into the air, the crowd roared with appreciation.

Most of the people in attendance recognized the mayor of Philadelphia, a swarthy Italian whose expressive gestures made him enormously popular. The mayor blew kisses back at the crowd as he accepted their accolades, taking credit for the event that was in its 94th year.

His appearance was Ophelia's cue to rendezvous with Lt. Governor Jay Rawlings in the office complex adjacent to the museum. They'd arranged for the interview to take place just as the parade disbanded. Rawlings wanted to keep it short. He'd scheduled lunch with the mayor right afterward.

Ophelia leaned toward Bella, who was snapping off pictures with her Nikon camera, and shouted in her ear. "Hey, I forgot to tell you that I'm supposed to interview someone right after this. It'll take me twenty minutes. Stay right here, and I'll find you when I'm done."

Bella's cherry-colored eyes widened with alarm. "Why can't I come with you?" she asked. "The parade's almost over."

Figuring Bella wouldn't take no for an answer—those DeInnocentis were so damned stubborn—Ophelia conceded with a shrug and led the way down the museum steps and across the street to an office complex leased by the environmental advocacy group that Rawlings chaired.

As they approached the building number Ophelia was looking for, a man wearing a wool trench coat, his cheeks ruddy from the cold, studied her approach with a hopeful look. "Ophelia Price?" he asked. She had kept her maiden name for the sake of simplicity.

"Yes." Adopting the demeanor of a top-notch reporter, Ophelia extended a hand. "And you are?"

"Dave Collum. I'm Jay Rawlings' assistant. He's expecting you." His tepid smile faded as his dark eyes shifted toward Bella. "I understood it would only be you."

"Oh, this is my camera woman," Ophelia asserted, thinking fast. "With the lieutenant governor's permission, we'd like to film the interview."

Collum's gaze fell to the Nikon camera hanging on a strap around Bella's neck and he shrugged. "It's up to him," he decided, pulling open the door behind him. "Follow me."

They stepped into a wide, echoing stairwell blessedly warmer than it was outside. Chatting about the weather and the magnificent parade, they climbed marble steps to the second level and stepped into a dark, deserted hallway and through a set of double doors. Ophelia's gaze lit immediately upon Jay Rawlings, who rolled out of the chair he was lounging in, fixed a plastic-looking smile on his face, and said, "Ah, here she is."

"I hope I didn't keep you," Ophelia apologized, taking a mental snapshot of his overall physique. The lieutenant governor was built like Vinny, only taller. The former Marine claimed the body of a much younger man, with broad shoulders and hewn thighs. While he admitted in his bio to having served in the CIA after his stint in the Marines, he'd never been forthcoming about the type of work he'd done for the Agency.

"Not at all. I just sat down. That was quite a parade, huh?" His astute gray eyes swiveled in Bella's direction.

Ophelia made introductions. "This is my camera woman, Bella. She's an intern."

"I didn't realize you'd be filming me." Jay Rawlings smoothed his thinning hair. "I thought this was just a write up for a Virginia paper."

She'd misled his secretary intentionally. And while Ophelia meant for this interview to be little more than a fishing expedition, filming Rawlings' reactions to her questions might be just what she needed to convince her boss to grant her exposé extra air time. "Well, no, I work for a news station—WTKR. We're located in Norfolk with a large military population."

"I see." His plastic smile returned as he gestured to the seats behind them. "Should we have a seat or do this standing up?"

"Let's sit," Ophelia said, shimmying out of her coat to reveal her striking outfit, one that Vinny hadn't noticed her leaving in as he'd already been hard at work on the washer in the basement. She tossed her coat over a chair. "Bella, you can stand over there and wait for my cue to start filming."

Playing right along, Bella moved wordlessly against the wall and fiddled with her camera settings. Ophelia applied herself to putting Jay Rawlings at ease. "Did you bring your family with you?" she inquired. Rawlings' offices were in Harrisburg, the state capital, an hour away.

"No, they had to stay at home. My son has a bit of a cold."

"Oh, what a shame," she lamented. "I bet your little boy would have loved the parade. That Santa Claus was very convincing."

They chatted for another minute before Ophelia cued Bella with a nod to start filming. "Well, thank you for taking time out of your busy schedule to meet me," she began, crossing her legs and shifting her body to display her cleavage to its best advantage.

"My pleasure," the lieutenant governor replied, brandishing his false smile. His gaze dipped automatically downward.

She'd worn her sexiest Jones of New York, java-colored wool suit. Tailored to show off her curves, it buttoned just below her breasts, which buoyed over the plunging neckline of her crème silk blouse. Tucking a curl behind one pearl-studded earlobe, she launched into introductions for the viewer and offered up standard questions, which the lieutenant governor answered with practiced ease. He was just beginning to look more confident when she brought up his service in the CIA. "Is it true that you worked for the CIA right after 9/11?"

The split-second pause on his part bespoke of his surprise. "Well, yes. After my service in the Marines, I still wanted to serve my country. 9/11 was a shock to all of us," he replied.

Another practiced answer, she decided, narrowing in for the kill. "Whatever made you leave the CIA?" she queried.

"Well, I, uh…I decided I could do more for Americans by working in politics."

"Then your decision had nothing to do with an operation in Basrah that went terribly wrong?"

The glint entering his gimlet eyes had an instant cooling effect on her body as he took a closer look at her, perhaps just now realizing that she wasn't your average, everyday reporter. He shook his head, "I'm sorry, but I don't know what you're talking about."

"August of 2002," Ophelia prompted, laying a hand on her cheek as if searching her memory.

"You'd been put in charge of an assassination attempt on Gabir al Baldawi, a radical Islamic leader believed to have dealings with Osama bin Laden. He was supposed to be holed up in a private home on the west side of Basrah. You were working with a small group of Navy SEALs. You raided the building, only al Baldawi wasn't there, just five or so civilians, including a boy and his mother who ended up dead."

Jay Rawlings had stiffened with every word coming out of her mouth. "Who told you this?" he growled, fighting to keep his expression pleasant.

Ophelia shrugged. "Like I said, I live in a military community, and that's the rumor that's circulating. Can you confirm or deny the story? Maybe you could clarify what went wrong?"

The lieutenant governor's expression grew subtly harder. "There's not an ounce of truth to that story. I never headed up an operation like that in Iraq. I don't know where you get your information, but I'd advise you not to listen to rumors that aren't true."

"I see," Ophelia said, with false sympathy. "So, this is just another attempt to discredit you in the eyes of the public. After all, you're being considered for the vice presidency." She raised her eyebrows at him. "It's amazing what stories the opposition will come up with in the hopes of ruining your reputation."

"That's true," he conceded, seizing on to her excuse. "The opposing party will do whatever it takes to bring me down. I assure you, I have never taken part in any military operation that I wasn't proud of. Of course, I'm not at liberty to talk about it these days, but my conscience is clear. I don't believe in keeping secrets."

"I didn't think so," Ophelia said with a reassuring smile. She signaled to Bella to stop filming and uncrossed her legs. "It's been a pleasure talking to you, sir. I hope we can do it again sometime," she added, holding out her hand to him. His palm, she thought, felt distinctly clammy as he squeezed her fingers briefly. The next time they spoke, she vowed she would have the proof to call him a liar. Any man that lied about his past had no business becoming the vice president of the United States. "Enjoy your lunch with the mayor," she added, pushing to her feet.

"Thank you," Jay Rawlings muttered, following her lead more slowly.

Gesturing with her head for Bella to start for the door, Ophelia retrieved her coat from the chair and threaded her arms quickly through it. "Have a wonderful Thanksgiving, gentlemen," she said. "We'll see ourselves out."

The staff member looked to the lieutenant governor, who nodded his agreement. Obviously, he wanted his man to stay behind so he could talk to him.

Ophelia's grin broke free as she and Bella stepped into the hall. Bella headed for the stairs, but Ophelia caught her by the arm, shook her head, and dragged her down the hall and around a corner. "Let's wait here," she hissed, tucking them both out of sight.

The look Bella shot her reminded her so much of Vinny that she could almost hear him saying, *Are you crazy?*

"I want to hear what they're saying on the way out," Ophelia explained.

"What if they catch us?" Bella's wide eyes shone with worry.

"We'll say that you had to use the ladies room."

"Me?"

"You're an intern. Interns do stupid things," Ophelia reasoned.

Bella rolled her eyes and huffed out a breath.

Down the hall, the office door clicked open. Ophelia peeked around the corner and snatched her head back. The lieutenant governor was stepping out of the room with David Collum on his heels, looking distinctly red-faced. Rawlings had taken his wrath out on the hapless man.

"I want to know who's talking to her." Jay Rawlings' distinctive voice echoed down the hallway.

"Another one of those goddamn SEALs has broken the code of silence."

"I thought we already took care of the leak," his staff member muttered.

"Quiet!" Rawlings grated. "Nobody needs to know about that. Maybe they're all talking. I don't know." Their heels echoed on the stairs, the door clanged shut behind them, and then they were gone.

Ophelia rounded on Bella "Did you hear that?" she cried, resisting the urge to jump for joy. "He just admitted to his involvement. I heard him!" But she had yet to find the proof. That would involve twisting the arms of some of Vinny's teammates, who had a tendency to clam up whenever she came around.

"We gotta get out of here," Bella told her with a tremor in her voice.

"Yeah, yeah. In ten minutes, so we know that they're good and gone."

Bella turned her eyes toward the ceiling and the discreet, domed camera overhead. "There's gotta be security in this place, even on holidays," she agonized aloud. "I can't afford to get arrested. I'll be thrown out of school."

Doubt pricked Ophelia briefly. "You're the one who insisted on tagging along," she said, turning the blame back on her sister-in-law. "Fine, we'll leave right now," she conceded as Bella started wringing her hands. "The secret is to act like you belong. Shoulders back, head up. Let's go."

Together they marched down the hall toward the stairs that the men had taken, but two silhouettes remained visible through the glass inset on the other side of the door. With a gasp, the women retraced their steps.

"Let's find another way out," Ophelia suggested, pulling Bella behind her as they searched the maze of hallways for another set of stairs. At the back of the building, they discovered an interior fire exit and took it to the lower level. Ophelia's gaze alighted on a sign that warned that an alarm would go off if the door were opened, and her confidence wavered.

Bella whirled on her. "Great! What do we do now?"

"We'll make a run for it," Ophelia decided. "The streets are crawling with people. Who's going to see us if we blend into the crowd?"

"Fine," Bella conceded, but her face paled with worry.

"Listen, we had every right to be in the building, and now we're leaving," Ophelia assured her. "It's no big deal. Come on. Just follow my lead. Act casual." Throwing her weight into the door, she pulled Bella out into the cold with her. They made a beeline toward the street that was teeming with people. For several seconds, only the sound of voices, traffic, and a flute being played by a home-less woman filled the air. But then the door clicked shut behind them, and a high-pitched wail floated from the building, alerting the world to a breach.

Ophelia snatched up Vinny's sister's hand and guided her briskly along with the throng heading toward the Philadelphia Art Museum.

Bella's fingernails dug into Ophelia's palm, but no one pursued them. No one shouted, "Hey, wait!"

"See, I told you we'd be fine," Ophelia said, free-ing herself from Bella's death grip as they picked their way across the steps toward the opposite side of the museum. It was there that they had parked Bella's car, in the hotel parking garage where her boyfriend worked as a valet.

Bella searched the faces in the crowd before glancing sharply at Ophelia. "Let me guess," she drawled. "You don't want Vinny knowing anything about this."

"Right. And if you tell him," Ophelia warned, "then I won't give you the iPad I bought you for Christmas."

"What?" Bella cried, startling to a halt. "You bought me an iPad?"

Well, she hadn't done it yet, but she intended to. "Yes."

"Oh, my God, you are such a great sister-in-law. Crazy but great," Bella amended, throwing an arm around her as they proceeded to their destination. Her expression grew reflective. "And, by the way, that guy was totally lying about that op, wasn't he?"

"He admitted it on the way out," Ophelia reminded her. "Now all I have to do is prove it."

"YOU HEAR THAT?" Jay Rawlings paused at the point of climbing into his chauffeured Town Car to look up at the high-rise building they'd just come from.

"It sounds like the alarm's going off," said his assistant, looking nonplussed.

"Why would the alarm be going off? It never did that before."

Dave Collum stared back at the building, looking flummoxed.

"Well, don't just stand there," Jay snapped. "Go shut it off."

"Sir," the man protested, turning back to him, "the alarm goes off when the fire door at the back of the building is opened."

"But that's impossible. The women left out the front, ahead of us."

Collum's eyes widened as he stared over the top of Jay's car. "Oh, no, they didn't. Look." He pointed to the crowd moving across the steps of the art museum. "There she is, right there."

Jay turned and searched the crowd. Within seconds, he spied the woman's coppery head as she sought to put distance between herself and the building, flanked by her dark-haired intern. Jay's eyes narrowed with suspicion. The conniving bitch! She only pretended to empathize with him about the rumor now circulating. She fully believed those rumors. What's more, she hung around after the interview, hoping to overhear something incriminating. He cast his thoughts back to the words he might have said on his way out.

Oh, Christ, he'd been mentioning the leak he'd already taken care of. He'd even brought up the possibility of another leak.

"Shit," he hissed. "Don't take your eyes off her!" Shoving his staff member in the right direction, he leapt into his car. "Follow her on foot and call my cell when you know which way she's headed. Mason," he said to his elderly African-American chauffeur, "drive straight ahead, slowly, and await my orders."

Leaving off his seatbelt to retain a hundred-and-eighty degree visual, Jay gripped the seat in front of him as they eased into traffic. Not thirty seconds later, his cell phone buzzed. "Which way?" he demanded, recognizing his assistant's number.

"They're crossing Pennsylvania Avenue, heading toward Fairmount," Collum relayed, huffing to keep up.

Jay issued Mason the order to hang a right. "Slower," he added, unnecessarily. The roads were jammed with cars leaving the area. They couldn't do more than creep forward one yard at a time. "Stay on the line with me," he ordered Collum. "Don't fucking let them get away. I want to know where that reporter's staying."

"Maybe at the Best Western. She's headed right toward it. Or, maybe not," Dave added a minute later. "They're going into the parking garage."

Jay raked an eye over the façade of the monstrous hotel in front of him. "Where's that?"

"Right side of the hotel." Collum panted into the phone with the effort it took to keep up.

"We'll wait outside on the street until she exits," Jay decided. He ordered Mason to pull into a handicapped parking space. Collum would blow it for him if he showed his face. "Don't let her see you," he warned into his phone. "If she drives by you, duck behind a car. I'll be right there to pick you up."

"Don't worry, sir. They haven't seen me yet. Looks like they're getting into a lime green Escort. You can't miss them when they pull out."

"Back off and wait at the opening of the parking garage. We'll get you on our way by."

"Yes, sir."

Jay put his phone away. Blood thrummed through his arteries; a muscle ticked in his cheek. Operation Lights Out had haunted him from the night it totally backfired. He didn't know if he'd trusted the wrong sources or if the assets he'd courted for six months prior to the operation had betrayed him, but either way, he'd fucked up. Gabir al Baldawi hadn't been in the apartment building surrounded by his closest advisors. Instead the place had been occupied by nothing but civilians. In his outrage he'd shot some kid who wouldn't stop wailing. The bullet had gone straight through him killing his mother, too—so what? Shit happened. He'd talked the SEALs he'd worked with into reporting the incident as an accident—either that or it'd be his word against theirs. They'd only agreed to keep silent if *he* agreed to leave the Agency.

He'd done what they wanted, so why the hell were they betraying him now? Jealousy, no doubt. Maybe they didn't want him being their vice president one day.

The vision of a lime green Escort snapped him out of his cold sweat. "Follow that car, Mason," he said, pointing it out.

As his chauffeur pulled away from the curb, Jay spared a glance at Collum, who stood near the parking garage expecting to be picked up. "Leave him," Jay ordered as the Escort gained speed, threatening to slip out of sight. Ignoring Collum's look of dismay, Jay focused his attention on keeping the smaller car in sight.

Two intersections away, the women's car bore right on Arch Street and disappeared. "Drive faster," he bit out. They turned the corner just in time to see the Escort veering toward South Broad. When they caught sight of it again, it was turning left onto Christian Street, making its way into the old, Italian neighborhood of Bella Vista.

A block ahead of them, it parallel parked in front of a series of row homes. "Pull over," Jay hissed at Mason. "Don't let them see us."

Mason swung the front of the Town Car into the nearest alley, leaving the back end sticking out. Jay craned his neck and watched the two women get out of their vehicle and hurry into the one brick house that had been painted pale yellow. He waited another five minutes to see if they would emerge again. When they didn't, he instructed Mason to drive past the house.

The number on the door made it easy to find again—769. Now he knew where the reporter was staying.

"Sorry for the detour, Mason," he apologized, sitting back in his seat. "We can return for Collum now."

With his jaw muscles jumping, Jay considered what to do about the journalist. If he let her live, she could ruin his bid for the vice presidency. He would have to silence her the way he'd silenced the first Navy SEAL to betray him. And what about the intern? She would have to disappear, as well. He winced at the financial implication. Getting rid of people in ways that couldn't be traced back to him cost a lot of money. *Damn it!*

As they slowed at a stop sign, Jay roused from his dark thoughts and glanced at his watch. "Aw, hell," he growled. "Now I'm late for lunch with the mayor!"

CHAPTER THREE

VINNY STEPPED OUT of the basement, intent on washing up for the Thanksgiving meal when the words "former Navy SEAL" had him turning toward the tiny television perched on one end of the counter. Ophelia, Bella, and his mother heard it, too. The kitchen, which had been bustling with activity resulting in the mixed aromas of roasting turkey, boiling potatoes, and simmering cranberries, fell quiet as they all turned to hear the news story.

"...The rash of break-ins attributed to a gang of teens resulted in his death. John Staskiewicz left the Navy SEALs six years ago, returning to Fishtown, the neighborhood he grew up in." The photograph of a handsome man in fatigues appeared on the upper right side of the screen. "This is the first time that the break-ins have resulted in murder. Staskiewicz was shot in the head while sleeping. Anyone with information pertaining to his death is requested to call the police. Back to you, Chris."

As the anchorman moved on to a new topic, Ophelia turned three quarters to send Vinny a searching look. "Did you know him, honey?" she asked, probably noticing his incredulity.

He shook his head. "No, not personally." But he could have sworn he'd just seen that distinct name written somewhere. And then it came to him. It'd been scribbled onto one corner of a rectangular brown box sitting on the corner of his commander's desk. He'd seen it there two days ago when he'd dropped by to pick up his letter of recommendation for medical school. Having a photographic memory, Vinny was confident that the name was the same. And now the man was dead. But if the police thought some young petty thieves had shot a trained Navy SEAL in his sleep, they were seriously misled. He filed the incident away in his head to discuss with his commander later.

"Food's almost ready, *figlio*. Go wash." His mama shooed him out of the kitchen.

Ophelia trailed him into the empty hallway. "Did you manage to fix it?" she asked about the washing machine.

"Not yet." He made a face and showed her the grease under his nails. "I gotta get a new part tomorrow when the stores reopen, but at least I know what's wrong with it." He massaged the kink he'd gotten in his neck from craning to see up inside the bowels of the old appliance. "It needs a new tub bearing. Then the cylinder won't wobble like it's demon-possessed."

"You're so clever," Ophelia praised. Stepping closer, she whispered, "Did she confide in you about her health?"

Fixing the machine had been easy. Getting his mother to admit that she needed to see a doctor wasn't. Vinny grimaced. "Not really. She said she was afraid the doc would tell her the cancer was back." His chest tightened at the possibility. "I made her promise to make an appointment next week. How was the parade?"

"Great," she said a tad too brightly.

Something about the way she said it roused the suspicion that she was hiding something, but he couldn't imagine what. "Okay," he said searching her turquoise eyes for clues.

But she turned away, going back to help his mama before he could query her further. With a shrug, Vinny hurried upstairs to shower and change.

By the time he rejoined the women, the kitchen table had been set with a lace tablecloth and his mama's finest china. The food lay along the counter like a buffet.

"Cut the turkey, *figlio*," Mama ordered. "S'time to eat!"

Vinny obliged, slicing up the turkey with a knife in bad need of sharpening. Mama led them in a blessing and then they piled their plates with food and sat down to enjoy it.

Mama Rose sent a critical look at Lia's plate. "That's all you eat?" she demanded.

Lia looked down at her plate and up at Vinny. She had loaded up on green beans and white meat, the kind of lean foods she usually ate to keep her figure trim for the cameras.

"She'll get seconds, Mama," he assured her. "Have some cranberry sauce on your meat," he suggested, passing Lia the cut glass relish plate.

Lia took the plate with an inscrutable expression, dished up a spoonful of sauce and plopped it next to her meat.

"Potatoes," Mama insisted, frowning critically at her daughter-in-law. "How you supposed to make babies when you so skinny?"

"Mama," Vinny interjected on a warning note.

"I'll eat her portion of the potatoes," Bella offered. "And her portion of pie, too."

"Oh, no you don't." Lia surprised them all by leaping to her feet and spooning a heaping mound of mashed potatoes onto her plate, then dousing it with gravy. Vinny held his breath as she retook her seat. Was she playing games? he wondered. Calling his mama's bluff?

To his surprise, she proceeded to eat every last bit of food on her plate. She even ate a bite of his pumpkin pie.

An hour later, they lay across his bed, too replete to do anything but rest for a while. Lia lay with her head on Vinny's chest, talking on her cell phone to her sister, and then to her three-year-old nephew, Ryan.

"Is Joe there?" Vinny asked, wanting to speak to his commander. With a curious glance at him, she asked Penny if she could put Joe on the phone, and then she relinquished her phone to her husband.

"Happy Thanksgiving, sir," Vinny greeted his commander and brother-in-law with mixed familiarity and formality. "How's it goin'?"

"Very well. And you?"

"Excellent, sir. My mama outdid herself this year."

"So did Penny. We've got my folks visiting."

"That's what I heard." He decided to cut to the chase. "Actually, I have a question for you. Did you ever know a SEAL named John Staskiewicz?"

The silence on Joe's end supplied an answer even before Joe confirmed it. "Yes, we served on Team Three together. Why do you ask?"

"You know he's dead, right?"

"What?"

Joe's outburst betrayed shock. "I'm sorry," Vinny apologized. "I just heard it on the news. He was supposedly killed by some teenaged thugs who've been breaking into houses, but I think that's bullshit." Realizing that his wife was listening avidly to their conversation, Vinny transferred the cell phone to his other ear to mute Joe's side of the conversation.

"When was this?" Joe asked him, sounding more concerned by the second.

"Just last night, I'm guessing," Vinny replied. "I saw his name on that box on your desk."

His commander heaved a sigh. "Listen, Vinny." Vinny could hear him withdrawing to a private area of his house. "What I'm about to tell you stays between the two of us. Can Lia overhear us?"

Vinny glanced down at Lia to assess how much she was hearing. She'd closed her eyes with her head on his chest, pretending to doze, but he could tell that she was straining her ears to hear, though he was fairly sure she couldn't. "No, sir."

"John and I worked together about ten years ago, along with Senior Chief McGuire and Chief Harlan. I was their OIC in a firing squad sent to Basrah to eliminate a high-profile terrorist. We worked under the direction of a CIA case officer, who must have gotten his intelligence wrong because the target wasn't in the building we hit, just a bunch of families, mostly women and kids. One kid wouldn't stop crying and the case officer wigged out and shot him. The bullet pierced the kid and killed the mother, too."

"Jesus!" Vinny exclaimed with disgust for the man's brutality. If Lia hadn't been listening intently earlier, he knew she certainly was now.

"Then he threatened to turn the tables on us if we reported him, so we made him a deal. We'd write off the incident as an accident if he promised to leave the Agency. We thought that would be the end of it. But then he went into politics. He's the lieutenant governor of Pennsylvania now, Jay Rawlings."

"No shit," Vinny breathed.

"And he's on his way to becoming the vice president. When John realized that fact, he decided to go back on his word and write an exposé. Now you're telling me John's dead."

It was Vinny's turn to be shocked into silence. It looked like the SEAL had been murdered—not by teenaged thugs but by a powerful politician determined to safeguard his reputation. "So, what are you going to do with that box, sir?" he finally asked, careful not to mention John's name, lest Lia put two and two together.

"I think I need to turn it into NCIS and let them investigate. Thanks for telling me about John. I think I'll make some phone calls now to find out when his funeral's taking place and where. I'd like to attend it."

"Well, keep me posted if it's somewhere in the area."

"I'll do that, Vinny. Thanks for the phone call."

"I'm sorry about the news, sir."

"Yeah, it's pretty sobering. I'll see you soon, Vinny."

"Have a good evening, sir."

No sooner had Vinny hung up than Lia's head popped up. She propped a hand under her chin and searched his gaze avidly. "How well did he know him?" she inquired.

Vinny pretended ignorance. "Know who?"

"The SEAL who was killed, of course. Did they work together?"

Vinny shrugged. "He said he'd worked with the guy back in Iraq."

"Hmm." She didn't look too surprised to hear it. With only 2,500 active duty SEALs worldwide, most SEALs had at least heard of each other. "But he hadn't been informed of this Stasky-guy's murder," she accurately guessed. "Did he mention if he had any enemies?"

"Staskiewicz," Vinny corrected.

She frowned at him. "Don't change the subject. What aren't you telling me?" she demanded.

He heaved an exasperated sigh and closed his eyes. "You know I can't talk about certain stuff," he admonished.

"But this is a civilian matter," she reasoned, "because Staskiewicz retired from the teams, and *then* he was killed. The only reason why you couldn't talk about his death was if it related in some way to—Oh." She eyed him with dawning comprehension. "Joe thinks his death is related to the work he did in the Navy."

"I'm not sayin' if he does or doesn't," Vinny insisted.

"I'll torture you," Ophelia threatened, pinching the lean flesh of his abdomen.

"You can't break me," Vinny replied with confidence. "I've been trained to resist interrogation."

She nonetheless gave it her best shot, going up on her knees to tickle him mercilessly. He bore her attack for as long as he could stand it, then captured her wrists, flipped her onto her back, and rolled up and over her.

"Oh," she moaned, the color draining from her face. "I think I'm going to throw up."

He immediately eased his weight off her, watching with worried eyes as she rolled toward the edge of the bed and covered her mouth. "I'll get a trash can," he volunteered, springing from the bed to find it.

"No, I'm okay," she assured him. Breathing in through her nose and out of her mouth, she sat up slowly. "I just think I ate too much."

"You didn't have to do that just to please Mama."

"I know." She closed her eyes and gnawed a moment on her lower lip, making him think that she might say something more on the subject of his mama's overbearing attitude. "I think I'll take a nap," she said, instead. "All that turkey made me sleepy."

"Sounds good to me." He flopped back down on the bed and gathered her against him.

"You sure you won't tell me what Joe said?" she asked, nuzzling his neck in a last-ditch effort to break him.

"You're relentless," he noted without rancor. "Listen," he added, changing the subject before she could sink her claws into him, "I'm gonna put that new part in Mama's washing machine tomorrow morning, and then I think we should head home early to beat the traffic. That okay with you?"

"Sure." She settled herself more comfortably. "But I promised I'd take Bella to Macy's tomorrow, so I have to go shopping first. Their Black Friday sales are out of this world."

"Sounds okay," he agreed. "Just remember this city is bigger than what you're used to. You know how easily you get lost."

"Macy's is a mile and a half away, and Bella will be with me. I can't possibly get lost," she mumbled.

"Keep your phone on, all the same. That way I can find you."

"Stalker," she slurred sleepily. In the next instant, she issued a soft snore.

"ROBERT HAS THE day off," Bella relayed, having just checked the texts on her cell phone. She clutched the phone with a dejected look.

Ophelia was about to pull her Kia Soul away from the curb at Mama Rose's. With the heater in Bella's Escort on the fritz, she'd elected to drive her own car. Bella's regret-filled tone had her shooting her sister-in-law a sideways glance. "You want to cancel our shopping trip so you can be with him?" she asked, hesitating.

"No, that's okay. Vinny wouldn't want me ditching you."

"Hmm." Considering her options, Ophelia proceeded to pull out, speeding them in the direction of Macy's. The drooping corners of Bella's wide mouth made her recall how desperately she had longed to spend time with Vinny back when they were dating. "Well, what if Vinny never found out?" she proposed, arching an eyebrow at her sister-in-law as she neared an intersection.

Bella's dejection evaporated. "What do you mean?" Her eyes brightened hopefully.

Ophelia slowed at the intersection, looked both ways, and gunned straight through it before realizing she had run a stop sign—again. But then the car behind her did the same thing, making her feel a little less remorse. She was supposed to be turning over a new leaf for the baby.

"How about I drop you off somewhere close to Macy's?" she suggested. "Robert can meet you there, and you two can hang out while I shop. Then I'll pick you up again on my way home. Vinny will assume we spent the morning together." With an impulse to browse the maternity section, she had good reason for wanting to shop alone. "We won't even have to lie to him."

"Well, there's a Starbucks right across the street from Macy's," Bella considered out loud. "Maybe Robert and I could hang out there."

"Perfect," Ophelia agreed, darting a dirty look at the car that was riding her rear bumper. "I turn right here, don't I?" she asked as she neared a stoplight.

"Either here or the next light. Are you sure about this?" Bella sent her a searching look. "I don't want you to feel neglected or anything."

"Sure I'm sure. I remember what it's like to be in *love*." She waggled her eyebrows at her sister-in-law.

"That's because you and Vinny are still in love," Bella pointed out.

Ophelia smiled a dreamy smile. "True," she mused. Seeing the next light about to turn red, she slowed down instead of speeding up, and the car dogging her nearly plowed into her back end. *Watch it, asshole,* she almost yelled, but then she remembered that she'd met Vinny by crashing into the back of his Honda. It wasn't that long ago that she would have done the same thing.

Should she have told him about the baby last night? she agonized. Or was it better to guard her secret just a little longer and surprise him on Christmas morning as she'd planned?

"There's the Starbucks on the right." Unaware of Ophelia's private thoughts, Bella pointed to the familiar green sign looming over the sidewalk up ahead. "You can look for parking in the lot farther up Market Street. If that lot's full, go around Macy's and you'll see a Wannamaker parking lot. There ought to be some spaces left in there."

"I'll find something," Ophelia assured her, slowing next to the curb. "Out you go. Say hi to Robert for me."

"Okay. Call me when you're almost finished, and I'll meet you somewhere. You have my number, right?" Bella leapt out.

"I've got it." She stuck a hand out the window, waving for the driver behind her to go around, but he would rather beep his horn than change lanes. Bella shut the passenger door, and Ophelia swung back into her lane, punching the accelerator.

AS BELLA WATCHED her sister-in-law veer into the nearest parking lot, a belated sense of uncertainty pricked her. The driver who'd beeped his horn so rudely still followed right on Ophelia's bumper. Black Friday sales in Center City would make it hard to find parking. Lia, who had an abysmal sense of direction, could probably use her help finding the other lot. All the same, she dialed Robert's number and held her phone up to her ear.

"Hey, Bella." His beloved voice distracted her from her private concerns.

"Hey, guess what? I have a couple of free hours," she admitted, grinning at the prospect of spending time together. "Can you meet me at Starbucks in Center City?"

"Sure," he said. "Bet I can make it there in under twenty minutes."

"I'll time you." With a light step, Bella turned and waltzed into the café looking forward to his arrival.

LIA COULDN'T FIND a parking spot to save her life.

The same aggressive driver dogged her every move as she circled the lot on Market Street. After three unsuccessful tours of the full lot, she gave up and left in search of the Wannamaker lot. It was right where Bella had described it. At the back of that lot, still tailed by the other car, she spied a tiny space that had gone overlooked due to the oversized SUV's on either side hemming it in. Careful not to clip her mirrors, she swung her Kia Soul into the aperture, claiming it before the other driver could wrest it away.

"Hah," she exclaimed, turning off her engine. A glance in her rearview showed no sign of the other driver. "I win." Snatching her purse off the floor, she verified that her phone was turned on, her ringer set on high, and then she pushed out of her car intent on some serious shopping. A thumb swipe on the exterior handle locked her car up tight. She turned toward the exit for the short hike to Macy's.

She hadn't taken three steps when she collided with a swarthy, barrel-chested man rounding the

SUV parked to her left. "Oops. Sorry." Oh, God, it was the angry driver who'd been tailing her. He was probably going to chew her out for stealing the space.

To her astonishment, he threw his burly arms around her, whipped her back to front against his barrel chest, and jabbed something sharp into her upper arm, straight through the material of her lightweight coat.

Ophelia gasped in horror. The burning pinch of a needle made her realize she'd been injected. Sure enough, she looked down and saw a syringe in the man's hand. Seizing her purse from her limp grasp, he began dragging her back toward her car, her heels scraping over the concrete.

I'm being abducted! The realization preceded a humming in her ears. Darkness hovered at the fringes of her field of sight. She fought its encroachment, keeping her eyes wide open. Removing his hand from her mouth, the stranger unlocked her vehicle using the remote key in her purse to give him access.

Scream! Ophelia commanded herself, but her head lolled, suddenly too heavy to hold up, and a mere whimper vibrated her voice box.

With a dark snow falling before her eyes, she felt herself being lowered across the rear seat of her car. The man grunted, sliding her up until he could shove her feet inside the car and shut the door. Ophelia lay on her side, one foot on the seat, the other on the floor. *Stay awake!* she ordered herself.

The part of her brain still capable of functioning came to a bone-chilling conclusion. This wasn't some random abduction. This had to do with her interview with Rawlings yesterday—she just knew it.

He's going to kill me!

The startling insight preceded utter darkness. *Vinny!* Her heart cried out in remorse. She ought to have told him the truth—not just the truth about her interview with Rawlings but also the truth about their baby. Now, he would never guess what had become of her, unless Bella told him. *Oh, Bella, please tell Vinny. Tell him everything!*

CHAPTER FOUR

BELLA CONSULTED HER android, only to frown at the empty display. It was 12:15 P.M., and Ophelia had yet to call her. They'd promised Vinny that they'd be home by noon. At this rate, they would arrive home late, giving Vinny cause to worry for no reason.

"I'd better call her," she said to Robert, whose grimace told of his disappointment that their time together was dwindling to a close. Dialing Lia's number, Bella frowned when Lia's voice mail answered in lieu of a ring. A frisson of concern had her finishing her second cup of coffee in one big gulp. "Something's wrong. Her phone's not even turned on."

Robert gave a negligent shrug. "She's probably listening to the organ recital. Maybe they ask people to turn their phones off."

"Doubtful." Macy's giant organ, the largest functioning pipe organ in the world, gave a thunderous

Christmas recital every two hours during the holiday season. A ringing cell phone wouldn't begin to disturb the sonorous performance. Bella's phone buzzed and she immediately snatched it up, only to cringe as she recognized Vinny's number. "Hello?"

"Yo, where are you girls? You said you'd be home by noon. Mama's got lunch ready."

"Uh…" Dread put a cold spot on the top of Bella's head. "I'm not actually with Lia right now," she carefully admitted.

"What?" His confusion elicited a pinch of guilt.

"She…she said I could go to Starbucks while she finished her shopping, and I haven't heard from her since." The silence on Vinny's end had her holding her breath.

"When's the last time you actually saw her?" he demanded, apparently seeing straight through her prevarications.

"When she turned into the parking lot next to Starbucks," Bella confessed, tucking her chin in shame.

"Then you never actually saw her get out of her car?"

"No."

"Have you tried calling her at all? Has she answered her phone for you?"

"All I get is her voice mail. Maybe her battery died."

"She charged it all night. You were supposed to stay together," he added on a scolding note.

"Well, she's got Friend Finder on her phone. Can't we find her that way?"

"The app doesn't work when her phone's turned off. It put her last location at the Wannamaker parking lot."

At least that made sense. "She's bound to be here somewhere."

"Tell me you left your keys for the Escort here at the house," Vinny demanded.

"They're on my dresser," she told him.

"Good. I'm coming to pick you up. Wait right inside the door at Starbucks and keep trying Lia's number. Let me know if you get through to her."

"Okay." She ended the call and met Robert's worried blue stare. "You'd better disappear," she warned. "My brother's on his way and you don't want to meet him right now."

Robert looked puzzled. "Does his wife do this often?"

"Um, no, I don't think so. But I have a bad feeling about this." For some reason, her thoughts kept circling back to Lia's interview with Rawlings yesterday. If that man harbored a secret he thought Lia might reveal—a secret that could cost him the vice presidency—wouldn't he take measures to try and stop her? "You'd better go, Robert." She slipped off her stool, pecked his cheek, and went to wait by the door.

Out the corner of her eye, she could see Robert studying her in the same protective way that Vinny watched her. She dialed Lia's number again, to the same result. When her Escort drew alongside the building minutes later, she sent Robert an apologetic wave, dashed outside and slipped into the passenger seat.

The set of Vinny's jaw warned her not to speak unless spoken to. He wordlessly peeled out, turned left at the next intersection and headed for the Wannamaker parking lot. They circled it twice, keeping a sharp eye out for Lia's Kia Soul. It wasn't anywhere to be seen. Vinny braked next to the parking attendant's little hut. "Excuse me," he called through his lowered window. "Do you remember an orange Kia Soul entering or leaving this lot in the last couple of hours?"

"Uh, yeah actually." A young man with a bad case of acne leaned out of his window. "Some guy followed her in here. I figured it had to be her husband cause he drove off with her car and left his here."

"*I'm* her husband," Vinny snarled at the young man. "Show me where this guy's car is. What did he look like?"

A minute later, Vinny was walking around an ugly, beat up Volvo, memorizing every detail about it, and bending to inspect the plates. Bella hugged herself in her seat trying to quell the tremors that had started radiating from her belly. Vinny was calmer than she thought he would be. Being a SEAL must have taught him to control his Italian temper, but she would almost prefer to see him yelling and pitching a fit than looking gray around the gills, his eyes dark with confusion. What, did he think, even for one moment, that Ophelia had run off with another man?

"He switched the plates," Vinny volunteered, sliding back behind the wheel and gesturing to the back of the ugly sedan. He pulled out his cell phone.

Bella's gaze flew back to the plates on the Volvo. I XPOZ U. Now, why hadn't she noticed that? "Vinny, I have to tell you something," she volunteered, a shiver running up her spine.

At the verge of placing a call, he cast her a distracted glance. "What?"

"I might know who's behind this."

His dark pupils seemed to expand as they focused on her. She had his full attention now. "Talk," he ordered with so much intensity that she had to swallow to find her voice.

With their car fogging up as it idled in the parking lot, she relayed the story of their interview of

Rawlings the day before. The words tumbling out of Bella's mouth made Vinny more tense than ever. When she mentioned Rawlings' name, he turned as white as a sheet.

"Oh, Jesus," he moaned when she told him how they'd hidden in the office building and how they'd overheard Rawlings' assistant say that they'd taken care of the leak. "I filmed the whole interview. I have it at home on my camera," she added.

Vinny scrubbed a hand over his face. She thought he might call 9-1-1 as soon as he recovered or drive like a bat out of hell to their mother's house. Instead, he accessed his contacts on his phone and placed a call. "Sir," he croaked in a voice that radiated alarm. "Tell me you didn't give the book to NCIS yet," he pleaded.

Bella had no idea what book he was talking about.

"She interviewed him yesterday," he blurted, re-laying what she'd just told him to someone she figured he worked with. "And now she's missing— gone. Some guy grabbed her in a parking lot a couple of hours ago while she was out shopping. He took off with her in her car, but her phone's turned off, so I can't find her."

VINNY COULDN'T BELIEVE the words that were coming out of his mouth. He had to be dreaming. It wouldn't be the first time the risks Ophelia took left him bathing in a cold sweat. But if this was a dream, he wasn't able to rouse from it.

His CO's voice seemed to be coming at him from a great distance. "Call the police," Joe Montgomery urged, his calm, implacable voice helping to steady Vinny's thudding heart. "Tell them Lia's missing. Have them put out an APB on her vehicle and look for evidence, but don't tell them your suspicions about Rawlings or he'll find out that we're on to him. I was planning to fly up there for Staskiewicz's funeral tomorrow," Joe added, "but now I'll grab the first hop out of here, bringing Senior Chief McGuire and Chief Harlan with me. We'll come straight to you. In the meantime, I have an idea that should keep Rawlings from hurting Ophelia. I'll text you his response as soon as I get it."

"Thank you, sir." The phone clicked in his ear. In his shock, it took Vinny a second to recollect what to do next. With fingers that shook, he dialed 9-1-1.

Oh, God, Ophelia. Where are you?

To an apathetic operator, he reported Lia's abduction, said he would wait in the Wannamaker parking lot for the cops to come, and hung up.

Too overwrought to do anything but stare up at the overcast sky, it occurred to him that his whole world was falling apart, and he was helpless to do anything about it. The sound of Bella stifling a sob wrested him from his self-absorption.

"This is all my fault!" his sister wailed, burying her face into her hands.

He palmed the back of her head and pulled it toward his chest to give and receive a much-needed hug. "It's not your fault," he assured her while realizing that Bella might have been kidnapped, too, if the women hadn't gone their separate ways.

Hell, if anyone was to blame, it was Ophelia herself for refusing to recognize when she was out of her league. Exposing corruption was almost every bit as dangerous as killing or capturing terrorists. But whereas Vinny claimed the advantage of training and teammates, Ophelia worked utterly alone. Even when she ought to have told her husband what she was up to, she kept it to herself for fear that he would interfere.

Damn right he would have interfered. What the hell had she been thinking trying to pull Jay Rawlings off the pedestal he'd built for himself? Powerful men did not take lightly to having the skeletons pulled from their closets. Just look at what had happened to Staskiewicz. But then she probably hadn't made that connection between Rawlings and the former SEAL. He couldn't begin to wonder what was happening in her head right now. She had to be terrified…

He slammed a lid down on the errant thought that she might not even be alive. Of course she was alive. And if he and his commander had any say so, she was going to *stay* alive.

And if Rawlings dared to silence the wife of a Navy SEAL, then he would soon wish that *he* was dead.

"YOU HAVE A personal call on line three, sir." The voice of Jay Rawlings secretary and lunchtime playmate purred over the intercom on Jay's office phone in Harrisburg, Pennsylvania.

Personal call? Working his way through proposed legislative revisions, Jay tore himself from the tome before him. His heart gave a funny flip as he considered whether the call might have anything to do with Ophelia Price's disappearance—of course not. No one would have connected him to her abduction, and Collum would have called his cell phone, as he'd done earlier to report that only Miss Price had been abducted. She and her intern had split up, forcing their hit man to pursue just Miss Price. He would have to go back for the intern later.

"This is Jay Rawlings," he said, shaking off his prickle of concern and answering the call.

"Jay, this is a blast from the past. Joe Montgomery here. We worked together in Iraq when I was with SEAL Team Three. You knew me as Monty, remember?"

However friendly-sounding, the baritone voice of the golden haired lieutenant who'd followed his orders in Operation Lights Out doused Jay in an icy shock. "Monty," he stammered, finding with difficulty his usual glib tongue. "How the hell are you?"

"Well, I've been better, Jay. Don't know if you heard about it, but one of the guys in our old squad was murdered just down the road from you, in Philly—John Staskiewicz. Remember him?"

"Sure, I remember John. I hadn't heard that news. How awful. What happened?"

"Some thugs broke into his house and caught him off guard."

"That's terrible."

"Yeah, I'm on my way to his funeral. It's up in your neck of the woods. Now that you know, maybe I'll run into you there."

"Oh, well, I'll have to think about it. Awfully nice of you to pay your respects, though. I take it you and John have stayed in touch?" Christ, had all the SEALs collaborated against him and not just John? Was that how Ophelia Price had come to hear the rumors she'd mentioned? The phone went slippery in his sweating hand.

"No, not really," Monty said, leaving Jay weak with relief. "But, you know, we're a tight-knit community, which is probably why John left me this book that he'd written. I'm not sure what to do with it."

The blood in Jay's veins turned to ice as his greatest fears took fearsome form. That exposé that John Staskiewicz had threatened to write if Jay became the lieutenant governor must have made it farther than his computer, stolen and destroyed the night he'd been killed. Jay hadn't taken precautions soon enough. "Oh?" he said, his voice cracking.

"It's all about that op that went bad, Operation Lights Out," Joe added, confirming Jay's guess. "He described you as a cold-blooded killer, Jay. You know we SEALs take the code of silence fairly seriously, but John didn't care much for your politics. It's pretty clear he intended for his book to halt your ascent up the political ladder."

Jay swallowed against his dry throat. "What are you going to do with it?" he croaked.

"Well, that depends." Monty's answer made his heart thud uncertainly. "As it turns out, you've got something I need. Maybe we can come to an agreement."

"What have I got?" Jay swam in a cold sweat. The smooth talking SOB dared to blackmail him?

"The journalist, Ophelia Price. I'll give you the manuscript in exchange for her safe return."

"I've never heard of her." Jay pretended bafflement, even as the walls of his office seemed to shimmer like sand in the desert. How the hell had Monty put two and two together so quickly? Obviously the four-man firing squad he'd directed in Iraq had kept in touch all these years. What's more, they'd planned to expose him all along, involving the journalist to help them publicize their allegations.

"You know exactly who I'm talking about," Monty insisted. "Unfortunately, what you didn't know when you arranged to make her disappear, is that Ophelia Price is my sister-in-law."

"What?" Jay clapped a hand to his damp forehead.

"And as much as I'd like to honor John's memory by seeing his book published and your career go up in smoke, my wife would throw me out if I didn't get her sister back safe and sound. So here's the deal, Jay…"

With the phone clasped to his ear, Jay stared dazedly out the window praying for an acceptable ultimatum.

"You show up at John's funeral with Ophelia Price safely ensconced in your car; I'll show up with the manuscript, and we'll do a trade. How's that? You get to salvage your career, and I get to salvage my marriage. Fair enough?"

Jay gave one more stab at protesting his innocence. "I don't know what in hell you're talking about," he growled.

"Well, in that case, you leave me no choice. I'll make copies of the manuscript right now and mail them to *The New York Times* and *The Washington Post*. You'll be dead in the water by this time tomorrow. When Ophelia's body is found, you'll be faced with the death penalty, which I understand you supported in your bid for lieutenant governor. Good talking to you, Jay."

"Wait!" Jay blurted the word before he'd made a decision as to what to say, what to do. "How do I know you haven't made a copy of the book already, or that you won't expose me later?"

"Gee, I hadn't thought of that," Monty said with a heavy dose of sarcasm. "I guess you don't know. Either your career goes up in flames today or sometime further down the road. I'd guess the timeline's up to you. You have my number," the man noted. "Call me if you change your mind."

Pride kept Jay mute. He flinched as the phone clicked in his ear, signaling an end to the call. Numb with shock, he lowered his arm until the receiver clattered into the cradle.

His knees jittered as he stood staring at the gray sky outside. *What do I do?* There had to be a way to keep the past from haunting him, some way to alter records so that the exposé, if published, would look falsified. Jay still had friends in the CIA. Maybe one of them, with the right inducement, could hack into the mission files and alter the details, making Staskiewicz's allegations look like big fat lies, even if three other SEALs elected to corroborate them. But until Jay found an ally in the Agency willing to help him out, he had to get his hands on the manuscript before Monty sent it to the press.

With a shaking finger, he stabbed the intercom button. "Michelle," he rasped. "Get the last caller back on the phone with me, will you?"

"Of course. Just a minute, sir."

Brutally efficient, she got back to him in half that time. "Sir, I have Commander Montgomery on line one for you."

Jay snatched up the phone, hit line one, and with a bracing breath stated, "I'll see you at the funeral." With that, he hung up and lunged for his cell phone. His hands were shaking too badly for him to text David Collum, so he called him instead.

"Yes, sir?"

"I've changed my mind."

"What?"

"Call Fernando and tell him not to dispose of the package as planned. I need him to bring it to Philly on Saturday and hand it back to you."

"To me, sir?"

"Shut up and listen. Have him meet you at the usual spot at 8 A.M. Then bring the package to my Philadelphia apartment. I want it back in one piece with no marks on it, understand?"

"I guess." Collum sounded utterly confounded.

Jay ended the call. He could care less what Collum thought. For several minutes all he could do was to stand in one spot overcome by doubts. The jangling of his cell phone made him jump. "What?" Jay snapped, recognizing his assistant's number.

"He says his price is the same whether he brings it back or not. I said I would check with you first."

Jay ground his molars together. *The same?* Ten thousand dollars was a helluva fee for babysitting. But what choice did he have. He needed that manuscript. "Fine," he spat. "But only if the package is in *pristine* condition. And he can't be late."

"I'll tell him," Collum promised.

With a growl of rage, Jay hung up and hurled his cell phone across the room where it landed, by luck, on an armchair, bouncing harmlessly onto the Turkish carpet. Would this nightmare never end?

Air Force bombers dropped bombs on the enemy population and never got in trouble for it. So why should his knee-jerk action prevent him from attaining the vice presidency? It shouldn't. But silencing Ophelia Price the way he'd silenced Staskiewicz wouldn't keep the news of his actions out of the public eye, not anymore.

He didn't know how he'd do it, but he would have to find some other way to protect his reputation.

THE SOUND OF a rough male voice roused Ophelia from a drug-induced sleep. By sheer force of will, she slit her impossibly heavy eyelids, managing to glimpse the dark head of her abductor in the driver's seat before her eyelids slammed shut.

The man had been holding a cell phone to his ear. She could hear him talking. "My price is the same," he insisted, speaking with a Spanish accent.

His price. He was discussing his fee for disposing of her. *Oh, God. I'm going to die.*

A stifled whimper escaped Ophelia's unresponsive lips. The car seemed to lurch at the tiny sound she made. Fear gave her the strength to peer through her lashes again. This time she could see the driver angling his rear view mirror to look back at her, ascertaining whether she was surfacing from her sleep. She quickly shut her eyes again, playing possum.

How will he kill me? Quickly and painlessly, she hoped. Or would he torture her first to elicit the names of her sources? Of course, Rawlings already knew who the other SEALs were in Operation Lights Out, but he might wish to know if *others* knew. What could she say? She'd gotten her information by eavesdropping at her sister's Halloween party, where Joe and his senior chief had been reminiscing about past operations, not knowing that Ophelia lurked just around the corner, her ears pricked in hopes of hearing a juicy story.

As long as he doesn't name us in his book, John can say whatever he wants to, Joe had been pointing out. *What's he got to lose now that he's retired?*

True. And someone had better drag Rawlings off his mountain before he climbs any higher. The senior chief's voice grew rough with disgust. *I never dreamed he'd go into politics. Christ, I'll never forget the way he just turned and shot that kid and his mom like it was nothing.*

I hear he's on the short list for Vice President, Joe grimly volunteered.

Oh, Christ, no, Senior Chief protested. *Tell John to go ahead and write his book. Hell, I'll hand-sell it for him. We thought Rawlings was dangerous when he was working for the CIA? Wait until he's next in line to be our fucking Commander-in-Chief.*

Sudden insight cast a spotlight in Ophelia's head on a previously unrealized fact. This John that the SEALs had been talking about—could *he* be John Staskiewicz, the Navy SEAL who'd lived near Vinny, the one who'd been murdered? Was the world that small?

Oh, Lord, it was, wasn't it? In that case, they had all been on the op-gone-bad—Rawlings, Staskiewicz, Joe, Senior Chief, and one other SEAL. And when their target, Gabir al Baldawi hadn't been present in the building as expected, Rawlings had blown his top, shooting and killing some poor kid, along with his mother.

The SEALs had reluctantly agreed to cover up the truth. John Staskiewicz, the first to break his code of silence, had ended up dead.

Which meant that Rawlings would stop at nothing to keep the truth out of the public eye.

I am so dead, Ophelia thought.

Terror gave rise to a wave of nausea. Battling the urge to hang her head off the edge of the seat and vomit, she held as still as possible. If she so much as moved, her abductor might pull over and hit her with another crippling injection. God only knew what was in that stuff and what it was doing to the fragile little life in her womb.

My baby! Oh, God, she couldn't let her baby die with her.

As the car veered off the highway, banking onto a tight turning exit ramp, she adjusted her position surreptitiously. Their speed slowed, giving her hope that they would pull up to a gas station. But then she remembered—Vinny had topped off her tank right before arriving at Mama Rose's, three days earlier. Her gas-sipping engine wouldn't need fuel for several hundred more miles.

The car turned right, then left, before gaining speed and merging back into traffic. Had they switched directions, heading back the way they'd come? It seemed so, but that was unlikely. After all, her captor had a job to do, and he would see it through to its gory finish. The most that she could hope for was the chance to escape when he finally stopped.

CHAPTER FIVE

Aᴛ ᴛʜᴇ sᴏᴜɴᴅ of Vinny's cell phone ringing, the kitchen fell quiet. The eyes of the three Navy SEALs who'd just entered Vinny's mother's kitchen focused on Vinny as he glanced at his phone and took the call. "Hello?"

"Mr. DeInnocentis?"

"Yes."

"This is Sergeant Presti with the Philadelphia Police Force."

"Yes, sir." Vinny held his breath, praying for good news.

"Uh, unfortunately, there've been no reported sightings of your wife's vehicle. We can't treat this as a missing persons case until forty-eight hours have passed."

They didn't have forty-eight hours, but Vinny couldn't assert that without bringing up Rawlings' name. Thanking the officer for the call, he shooed his mother and sisters out of the kitchen and gestured for his teammates to sit. "You want any leftovers?" he offered belatedly, and they all shook their heads. He sent his commander an imploring look as they sat. "There's gotta be something we can do."

"There is," Joe Montgomery assured him. Lacing his big-knuckled hands on the table in front of him, he leaned in and pitched his voice lower. The SEALs had rallied around Vinny within hours of Ophelia's disappearance. A ray of late afternoon sunlight sliced through the window over the kitchen sink and emphasizes the disfiguring scar on Monty's otherwise handsome face. "Rawlings wants John's manuscript badly enough to trade Ophelia for it," he conveyed, causing Vinny to cover his eyes briefly to conceal his relief.

"Can we trust him to keep his end of the agreement?" he asked hoarsely.

Senior Chief gave a snort of derision.

"We don't have much choice," Joe replied, darting his senior chief a quelling look. "But that doesn't mean we're going to sit here with our thumbs up our asses. I've got a friend in the FBI—you know Hannah Lindstrom. She's monitoring Rawlings' phone calls as we speak. He's been talking to his assistant, David Collum, every few hours. Hannah suggested the three of us take off to Harrisburg tonight to keep tabs on both men. If they do anything suspicious, then we film them. It'll take convincing evidence to put a powerful man like Rawlings behind bars."

Vinny's temples throbbed. "I'm coming, too," he insisted.

"Negative." Joe fixed him with a stern look. "You're going to stay right here and protect your sister. Think about it: Rawlings has a motive for wanting her out of the picture, too. If he had Ophelia and Bella followed this morning, then he knows where Bella lives. You need to stay here to protect her."

Joe's observation pushed Vinny's concern to new heights. His commander was right. He had to think about his sister's and mother's safety, too. "You'll keep me updated," he pleaded.

"Absolutely," Joe assured him.

Vinny nodded. "Does Penny know what happened yet?"

"Not yet." Joe regarded him steadily. "You want me to tell her?"

Vinny pictured Lia's sister's reaction to the news. "No," he decided. The fewer people who felt as miserable as he did, the better. "We'll tell her tomorrow, when it's over." That was assuming everything went as planned—which it would, Vinny assured himself.

Joe sent him a sympathetic grimace. "I know what you're going through, buddy," he reminded his brother-in-law. "Believe me, when Penny was kidnapped by that thug working for the ricin thief, those were the longest twenty-four hours of my life. But if she managed to outsmart her kidnapper, who knows what Lia can do? She's hell on wheels when she makes up her mind to be; you know that."

Oh, he knew. And while Joe meant for his words to be reassuring, they only notched his anxiety higher. It would be so like Ophelia to undermine their rescue attempt by trying to escape on her own. The very real possibility that she could end up getting hurt, even killed, pushed tears of distress into his eyes.

Joe flicked a glance at his watch. "We should probably get going." He shoved his chair back, signaling to the others to do likewise. The diminutive kitchen could barely contain the four large men standing shoulder to shoulder.

"We'll see you at John's funeral." Senior Chief McGuire threw an arm around Vinny's neck in an uncharacteristic show of affection.

"Keep this," Sean Harlan said, pulling a Sig Sauer P226 out from under his T-shirt and laying it gently on the table, along with two boxes of extra ammo that he fished from his pockets.

Vinny reached for the weapon, still warm from Sean's skin, and tucked it into his waistband against the small of his back. "Thanks," he said, "all of you. I don't know what I'd do without you."

"Hell, you wouldn't be in this situation if it weren't for us," Joe pointed out.

That wasn't exactly true, Vinny ruefully reflected. It was Ophelia letting her professional ambition get the better of her common sense that had gotten them all involved.

Trailing his teammates down the hall to the door, Vinny let them out. He watched them slip into their government-issued sedan and drive away before shutting and locking the door and killing the lights.

Creeping up the stairs, he found his mother and sister consoling each other on his mama's bed. The picture they presented, crying and hugging each other, reminded him so forcibly of the night his father had abandoned them that he shut the door so he didn't have to see them. Then he made a perch for himself at the top of the stairs and waited. If Rawlings did send someone tonight to try to silence Bella, Vinny would be ready for him.

IT'S WEARING OFF again.

Ophelia blinked away the sticky weight that kept her eyelids shut. She lay face down across a soft surface, drawing on fractured memories of the last time she'd been conscious enough to make sense of her present situation.

She remembered the car stopping. The second the engine died, she'd sat up, determined to catch her captor off guard. Only, she hadn't moved fast enough. One minute she'd been pawing at the door handle, fumbling to release the lock, and the next she'd fallen into his arms. A light snow had flecked her cheek. She'd gleaned a fleeting impression of tall pine trees and cold mountain air just before the sharp prick of a needle pierced her shoulder for a second time. The last thing she remembered was being hauled out of the car and tossed over her captor's broad shoulder.

Where am I? A thread of faint silver light shone between two dark panels suggesting the presence of a window. Turning her head the other way, she spied a brighter beam of light at the bottom of a closed door. From beyond it came the sound of a television program, complete with canned laughter. The blanket under her nose emitted the odor of mothballs.

Given the bits of information at her disposal, she concluded she'd been driven to the Pocono Mountains. Was this where her captor meant to kill her, in some remote cabin where no one would hear her screams? If so, why hadn't he done it already? Perhaps he was waiting for her to regain consciousness. That made sense if he was after information.

Not going to happen.

She tried to move. Her limbs felt inordinately heavy from the drug still cycling through her veins. She discovered her feet bound, her hands also, with what felt like long plastic garbage ties. A numb fire licked up her arms to stab at her shoulder sockets. It was that pain that had roused her.

Stifling a moan, Ophelia rolled onto her back, jackknifed to a sitting position, and took closer stock of her whereabouts. The room appeared small but decently appointed—a dresser, a bed, and a mirror. Perhaps there was something she could use to cut herself free?

An object resembling her purse had her looking back at the dresser. Would her captor be so careless as to leave her purse, with her phone inside it, sitting right next to her?

Vinny! She could call for help.

Moving slowly, so as not to let the bed squeak, she stood up, not altogether certain her legs would hold her. When they did, she gave a little hop, and then another, leaned over the dresser and caught her purse between her teeth. She discovered the snaps hard to open without hands. The two halves of her purse parted at last beneath her wriggling jaw. She nosed her way into the main pocket, searching desperately for her phone. But it wasn't there. Her abductor must have removed it. He'd probably turned it off, too, so she couldn't be traced.

He wasn't careless after all. Or was he?

Seizing the whole bag with her teeth, she pivoted and dropped it on the bed, causing the contents to spill out. Then she sifted through them with her nose—makeup, checkbook, lipstick, ah ha! Fingernail file. She sat next to it, groping behind her back to pick it up. She would use it to cut herself free.

This looks a lot easier in the movies.

But hope and desperation lent her dexterity. Back and forth over the plastic strip she sawed, cutting through it one millimeter at a time. With a snap, the cuff around her wrists broke. Swallowing a cry of hope, she went to work on the strip that bound her ankles together. Outside her room, she could hear the television program give way to advertising. At any moment, her captor might get up and check on her.

Having injected her twice now, he was clearly cognizant of the fact that the drug only worked for a specific period of time. He was probably gearing up to inject her yet again—or worse yet, keep her awake for questioning and torture.

If it comes to that, I'll pretend I'm versed in torture like Vinny. But it wouldn't come to that if she could help it. She was getting the hell out of here before her captor could lay his hands on her again.

With another snap, the flex cuff dropped from around her ankles. Ophelia pushed to her feet. Straining to hear over her galloping heart, she dropped the file back into her purse along with the rest of her stuff, picked her purse up, and tiptoed toward the window. Discovering her coat hanging on the bedpost, she dove into it, fingers fumbling to button herself up. It would be cold out there.

She had just crossed the room to the window to further her escape when the television fell silent. Terror spiked, causing her to freeze like a thief, her ears pricked to the sounds beyond her door. Her captor seemed to be listening, also. Any minute now, he would get up to check on her. She couldn't afford to tarry.

Stretching out a hand that shook, she felt beneath the heavy curtain for a window latch. There it was, in the middle of the window, icy to the touch. The mechanism was simple and familiar. With a push of her thumb, she flipped it open, eliciting a scraping noise. On the other side of the door, the slow thud of approaching footsteps goaded her into reckless action. *Now, Ophelia!* She yanked aside the curtain, put both palms against the frosty pane, and pushed upward. At first it stuck. But then, with a pop, it rumbled upward, admitting a gust of frigid air that took her breath away. At least there was no screen to contend with.

The doorknob turned. *Should have locked that*, she realized in hindsight.

With the silhouette of her captor filling the opening door and his shout of warning abrading her ears, Ophelia threw herself head first out the opening, diving into the darkness. More than halfway out, her upper thighs caught on the windowsill. For a terrible second, she hung suspended, purse dangling from her elbow, her head mere feet from the dark earth while the man sought to grab her failing legs and drag her back inside.

With a mighty kick, Ophelia freed herself. Her captor's shout of pain echoed in her ears as she crashed onto the hard ground, hands outstretched to break her fall. A shooting pain radiated up her right arm just before the top of her head struck frozen soil. She tucked her chin, rounded her spine and rolled the way she'd seen Vinny do when he wrestled with her nephew.

To her amazement, she rolled right up on her feet. But she'd lost her purse in the tumble. No time to pick it up now. Clasping her right arm to her chest, she ran blindly into the shadows, only to discover that they were trees with sharp branches that clawed at her clothing and her hair as she wended her way through them.

The earth rose sharply under her Keds, forcing her to ascend a densely wooded slope, one with unseen boulders that jutted out of the earth causing her to trip. She fell to her knees, landed on a bed of pine needles, and struggled up again.

Behind her she could hear a door slamming and the tramping of feet.

As expected, her captor was coming after her. He'd seen which direction she was fleeing. She could hear him crashing through the forest in her wake, gaining on her steadily. She lengthened her stride, but he was frighteningly fast. *Hide!* She cast her gaze about, looking for a bush to squirm beneath, but the underbrush was tragically thin. Hearing him just feet away, she darted behind the wide trunk of a tree and froze.

He slowed, no doubt scanning the area, searching for her.

Ophelia fought to silence her panting. She could hear Vinny in her head, teaching her how to breathe the way Navy SEALs did—*Inhale for the count of three, through the mouth, hold for one second, slowly exhale.* But her chest convulsed in fear, causing her exhalation to come out in the form of a sob. Twigs snapped right behind her under the soles of her captor's shoes.

"Thought you could run?" He pounced without warning, prompting her scream of terror. "Shut up, *puta*."

The slap came out of nowhere, sobering her with its force.

"Come here." He grabbed her with impatient hands, whipping her around and prodding her back in the direction of the house. "You gonna get me in trouble," he groused in his accented English.

With her last shred of hope, she sought to outsmart him. "Whatever Rawlings is paying you, my husband will double it," she offered.

"I don't know who's payin' me, and I don't care."

"He's the lieutenant governor, Jay Rawlings."

"Shut up. I don't want to know nothin'. I just do what I'm told."

"Then you're nothing but a coward," she retorted.

"I said, *shut up*!" He gave her a push that sent her stumbling face-first into the nearest tree trunk. Rough bark scraped the side of her face, leaving it stinging. The injured hand she'd used to catch herself gave a throb of protest. "*Maricón*," he hissed, hauling her upright. "You gonna hurt yourself and I'll get the blame."

Mulling over his words, she winced as he grabbed her by the hair and propelled her toward her makeshift prison.

The cabin looked like something seasonal that a hunter might use. There were no other structures in sight—no signs of any other human inhabitants anywhere.

What did he mean he would get the blame for hurting her?

He shoved her through the open door, kicked it shut behind them and slammed her against the refrigerator. "Don' move," he warned, turning away to paw inside of a plastic case.

She touched a finger to her stinging face and realized it was bleeding.

When he turned around, her captor was sucking clear liquid from a capsule into a syringe.

"Oh, don't do that," she begged him. "You're going to hurt my baby with those drugs."

Dismissing her words with a sneer, he seized her shoulder and stabbed her through her coat like he'd done two times previously.

In the next instant, Ophelia slumped against him. As the room turned gray then black, it occurred to her that he was keeping her alive. But why?

CHAPTER SIX

"EAT YOUR SAUSAGE, *figlio*," Vinny's mother insisted.

"I'm not hungry, Mama," he said, ignoring his breakfast plate. He had stayed up all night guarding his family, and he still seethed with restless energy. With his mother puttering around him, he watched Ophelia's interview with Rawlings on the Nikon's previewer, unable to take his eyes off Rawlings—the slimy piece of shit. The man looked so clean-cut, so upstanding. To think that he could shoot a kid in the head just because he got on his nerves was bad enough; to have abducted Lia—Vinny's clever, glittering Lia—made Vinny want to wrap his hands around the man's neck and slowly squeeze the life out of him. Hell, that's what Rawlings was doing to Vinny, who couldn't think, couldn't breathe, couldn't even eat his goddamn breakfast because his wife was in peril.

Swallowing a bitter taste in his mouth, he wished that someone had tried to hit his house last night, after all. Not that he'd wanted Bella or his mother in harm's way, but he'd been stewing for a fight. Still was.

"Are you going to kill him?"

The fearful question brought Vinny's attention back to the present. He'd forgotten that Bella was sitting in the chair beside him, playing with her food. The dark smudges under her eyes and the pallor in her cheeks told him she had hardly slept a wink herself. "No," he told her, "'course not. I'm not a murderer. He's the murderer."

Bella nodded, her eyes watering.

"Hey," he said realizing she still blamed herself for everything. "This ain't your fault, Bella. No matter what happens, you remember that. Lia does what Lia does. You didn't force her into anything, did you?"

She shook her head, unable to answer him.

Just then his cell phone buzzed and he snatched it off the table, his pulse kicking to see that Joe was calling him. "Whatchu got, sir?" he demanded in lieu of a proper greeting.

"I saw her. She's alive."

"What?" Relief flooded his system, making him sink more heavily into his chair. "Where? How'd she look?"

"I've been tailing Rawlings' assistant, Dave Collum, while the others have been watching Rawlings." Considering how little sleep the CO had probably gotten, he sounded as sharp and on-the-ball as ever. "Collum left Harrisburg early this morning. I followed them to a warehouse over in South Philly, where a guy pulls up driving Lia's Kia Soul. The tags were different, but that dent where she backed into my mailbox is unmistakable. The assistant gets out, pays the other guy off, and then transfers Ophelia into his vehicle."

Vinny swallowed hard and repeated his second question through a tight throat. "How's she look?"

"Fine," Joe answered rather vaguely. "But listen up. I called the cops to report a sighting on the Kia Soul, so hopefully they've arrested her kidnapper by now. Chances are, he was the same guy Rawlings used to murder Staskiewicz. In the meantime, I've tailed Collum's vehicle to Rawlings' Philadelphia address. It looks like Rawlings plans to go through with the exchange."

Vinny scrubbed a hand over his face. His eyes burned with relief and the need to have Lia safe and sound and in his arms again, but it wasn't that easy.

"I want you to wear Harlan's dress whites at the funeral. Harley will be hiding so he can film Rawlings' actions during the exchange. The more evidence we can stack against him, the less chance he can get out of the charges we level against him later."

"Are you sure Lia's okay?" Vinny interrupted. Joe's refusal to elaborate earlier made him fearful. What wasn't Joe telling him?

"She's fine, Vinny. She appeared to be unconscious, which means he's probably got her drugged. There's a scrape on her face that Rawlings' assistant looked upset to see," he added on a side note, "but other than that, she's in one piece."

"A scrape. How bad of a scrape? Was she beaten?"

"I couldn't really tell. I was too far away. Listen, I gotta go. I'll see you before the funeral. We'll stop by your house to pick you up and head over in one car."

Severing the call, Vinny looked up to see his mother and sister staring at him with identical expressions of foreboding. "She's okay," Vinny relayed in a voice that was thick with relief. To his chagrin, he couldn't maintain his composure any longer. He covered his face with his hands and sobbed with relief. She was going to be back in his arms, back where she belonged by sundown. He could go on breathing.

Thank you, dear, sweet God!

LIA SURFACED FROM a deeply unconscious state, fighting the poison in her bloodstream long enough to determine where she was and what was happening to her.

Why am I naked?

Her sudden sense of vulnerability, a breath of cool air prickling her skin, heightened her awareness. She couldn't open her eyes—her abductor had clearly upped the dose of the tranquilizer—but she didn't have to see to know that she was being wiped down.

A wet cloth, smelling of urine and soap, moved briskly along her upper thighs, causing her to lurch reflexively. The surface under her back felt smooth yet hard, as though she lay on a sheet draped over a table.

"All done here," said a mature woman with an African American cadence to her voice. "Turn her over, Mason, and we'll clean her up from behind."

Appalled, Lia felt herself being flipped onto her stomach by hands that felt large yet feeble in contrast to her abductor's. *Who is touching me and why?*

The suspicion that she'd soiled herself made her face flame with mortification, but as she lay face down, those attending her didn't seem to notice. The woman resumed her no-nonsense job of tidying her up. "There. Now we can dress her again. Try not to stare, dear. What you ought to be doin' is asking yourself what this comatose woman is doing in our house."

"All I know is she's a reporter," answered an older man's voice. "She must have been trying to frame the boss or something."

The woman sniffed. "Well, if he don't have nothin' to hide," she pointed out, "then why's he doin' something like this? It's immoral, is what it is."

"Hush, now. The walls have ears," the man named Mason muttered. "He probably just means to teach her a lesson, is all. He's lettin' her go today. That's why we've got to dress her in clean clothes."

"Well, I will say this, Mason: Jay Rawlings ain't the man his father was. I think it's high time that you retire. I won't have you livin' out your days in prison, you hear? Now hand me those clothes and help me put them on her."

Ophelia seized upon the words the man had spoken—*he's lettin' her go*— and clung to them like a life raft. But then the weight of the drugs fouling her system tugged at her mercilessly, pulling her back under, into a sea of unconsciousness.

As THE GLEAMING, mahogany coffin began its descent into the gaping hole in the ground, the bagpiper, wearing a kilt that left his bare knees ruddy in the cold, drew a huge breath, inflating his instrument and filling the late afternoon stillness with a heartfelt tribute. A stiff autumn breeze forced the last golden leaf from the maple tree behind the bagpiper, sending it spiraling toward the grave and onto the lid of the casket, like Mother Nature's silent coda for the fallen soldier being laid to rest.

If anyone besides Vinny thought it odd that a man of Polish descent should be buried in a Lutheran cemetery to the strains of *Danny Boy,* they kept silent on the subject. For his part, Vinny was too busy trying not to jump out of his skin or vomit from anxiousness to question the strangeness of the proceedings. Standing by the graveside next to his CO and the senior chief, wearing Chief Harlan's dress whites and trying to appear calm, Vinny found this particular stakeout far more nerve-wracking than any mission he'd ever been on. The clear sky and the crisp November weather ought to have reassured him. Rawlings had arrived late to stand at the back of the assembled guests. Members of Staskiewicz's family had no idea that the man responsible for John's murder was even in attendance.

Throughout the ceremony, Vinny had fought the urge to shoot Rawlings malevolent glares. He'd satisfied himself by searching for Chief Harlan, who was staked out under a bush with the Sig Sauer P226 safely back in his competent possession. In lieu of the high-powered scope he usually used, Harlan lay at the viewing end of Bella's Nikon camera. Anything Rawlings said or did would be used to prosecute him to the fullest extent of the law.

At last, the coffin settled with a thud in its final resting place.

"Ashes to ashes," the pastor intoned, leaning over to pinch a bit of dirt between his fingers and toss it into the grave. "And dust to dust."

The family members lined up to follow his example.

With the bagpiper still wailing out the poignant melody, Vinny saw Rawlings offer a glib word to the man next to him and separate himself from the standing mourners. Vinny nudged his brother-in-law, who said out of the corner of his mouth, "I see him. Wait a bit."

Vinny ground his molars together. If he waited any longer, every black hair on his head was going to turn white.

The lieutenant governor had parked his car on the other side of the cemetery, far away from the other mourners. Joe waited for the man's silhouette to disappear behind a sarcophagus before muttering, "Now."

Together, he, Vinny, and Senior Chief McGuire broke away from the crowd and ghosted across the manicured grounds. The thud of Vinny's pounding heart echoed off his eardrums, muffling the crunch of dead grass beneath their feet as they threaded their way between the headstones.

Would Rawlings try to pull a fast one? Missing the reassuring weight of his MP5 submachine gun, Vinny wiped his damp palms on his thighs. This wasn't combat, but he felt the same way he did at the start of every op—sick to his stomach. Anything could go wrong, affecting the outcome of his life, dictating his destiny, threatening his identity as Ophelia's husband. His heart lurched with panic at the thought of losing her forever.

As a unit, they zeroed in on Rawlings' black Town Car, their steps measured and determined. The lieutenant governor lounged against his vehicle striving to look relaxed, but his gaze locked on Joe and then Senior Chief, and recognition flared in his gray eyes.

"So," he called when they ventured close enough to communicate, "we meet again." His voice dripped with disdain and with the condescending tone he must have used when guiding their actions ten years ago. "I always knew one of you would go back on your word."

"Is that why you had Staskiewicz killed?" Joe inquired for the benefit of Chief Harlan and his camera.

Rawlings sent him a sneer. "I don't know what you're talking about," he retorted. His gaze slid to the taped box tucked under Joe's left arm. "Is that the book?"

"Yes, it is." Nothing about Joe's voice betrayed his tension.

"Toss it over. Then I'll give you what you came for. And just so you know, if you plan to screw me over in the end, I'm taking you both down with me. You're both still active duty." He gestured at Joe and Senior Chief's uniforms. "How's it going to reflect on your careers if I allege that *you* were the ones who killed the kid and his mother? It's my word against yours, fellas, and I've got power on my side."

"I want to see Ophelia first," Vinny blurted. He didn't trust Rawlings not to jump into his car and take off, nor did he give a shit about what happened ten years earlier. He just wanted Ophelia back in his arms again.

Rawlings gestured for the book, and Vinny watched Joe toss the box onto the ground at the lieutenant governor's feet. Satisfied, Rawlings looked at Vinny as if seeing the young SEAL for the first time. "She's over there." He gestured to a looming statue of a shepherd holding a sheep.

Vinny pivoted, catching sight of a laced shoe peeking out from behind the statue and recognizing Ophelia's Keds in an instant. "Lia!"

He took off, not even waiting for Joe's permission, and raced with his heart in his throat toward the sprawled figure. She lay against the statue's base, her eyes half-open and glassy looking. One side of her cheek bore bruises and lacerations, although someone had done a fine job of cleaning her up. Her coat was buttoned to her chin, but he could see her shivering as he threw himself onto the cold ground, wrapped one arm around her, and reached at the same time for her pulse.

"I'm here, *cara mia*," he crooned, only vaguely registering the sound of Rawlings' car door slamming shut. An engine roared to life and faded into the distance. Guided by his training as a medic, Vinny fixed his attention on the faint pulse at Ophelia's wrist. Finding it swollen and bruised, he switched to the other arm. At the same time, a glance into her eyes confirmed that she'd been drugged.

Her eyelashes fluttered as she sought to focus on him.

"Vinny," she whispered. The tragic quality of her voice arrested him from counting her heartbeats. A single tear sluiced out of the corner of one eye. "I'm so sorry," she added, her words slurred.

"Hush," he exclaimed. "It's over. You're safe now, baby. No one's going to hurt you again."

At his assertion, her face crumpled into a picture of misery. With a cluck of dismay, he gave up trying to take her pulse, gathered her into his arms, and lifted her off the ground.

That was when he saw the blood. It had soaked the dead grass beneath the spot where she'd been lying. Horror electrified him. He searched automatically for a gun wound. Finding the hem of her coat drenched, he lifted it and realized she was bleeding *down there*. Jesus God, what had Rawlings done to her?

He turned a stricken face toward the SEALs who had already reached him, enclosing the grim scene of husband and fallen wife; Chief Harlan arrived a moment later looking uncertain as he clutched Bella's camera in his square hands.

"Call an ambulance," Vinny croaked in a voice he scarcely recognized as his own. "She's bleeding."

Commander Montgomery already had his phone out, his eyes sliding to the scarlet smear now staining the yellowed grass.

CHAPTER SEVEN

Lᴵᴬ ᴷᴱᴾᵀ ᴴᴱᴿ eyes closed, feigning sleep, even though the effects of the tranquilizer had finally worn off. Her sprained right wrist throbbed within the bandage that now kept it immobile. The sounds of the bustling hospital, audible through her closed door, reassured her that she was safe, no longer staring at her own imminent death.

Her pregnancy, however, had not survived the trauma, a fact that dragged her spirits down into a dark, muddy place where her conscience pointed the finger of blame squarely at herself.

She didn't have to open her heavy eyes to know that Vinny was sitting in the chair next to her bed, his brooding gaze on her face. She could sense him there, staring at her, willing for her to wake up so they could talk. Except, she didn't want to talk because then she'd have to accept her guilt and deal with it.

Talk to him, you coward, her conscience commanded.

It wasn't fair to Vinny to leave him just sitting
there, awash with confusion. She owed him an
explanation. She owed him way more than that, but
it was too late now.

Dreading the conversation to come, she drew a
bracing breath, forced her eyelids to open, and
turned her head to meet his bloodshot gaze.

God, if he looked *that* bad with deep brackets
around his mouth and dark circles under his eyes,
then she had to look a total wreck. "Hey," she
greeted him, in a voice scratchy with disuse.

His gaze seemed to tunnel through her eyes into
her mind. "Hey, yourself. How're you feelin'?"

"Sore," she admitted, swallowing against a dry
throat. "Could I have a drink of water?"

He handed her the large plastic cup off the
wheeled tray, and she whispered her thanks, nursing
the chilled water from the straw while she formulat-
ed what to say to him. She thought she recalled
apologizing at the cemetery when they'd been
reunited, but one apology scarcely atoned for the
enormity of her sins. She didn't know where to start.

"How long did you know?" Vinny demanded,
diving right in. A muscle jumped in his jaw as he
awaited her answer.

The reminder that the precious little life she'd been guarding was gone drove a shaft of pain straight through her heart. She lowered the cup to her lap and stared down at it, devastated. She had tried turning over a new leaf. She had wanted to put the baby first, and now it was too late. "Almost two months," she admitted, too ashamed to even look at him.

Stunned silence followed her reply. "*Two months*," he finally repeated, in a voice that resonated with betrayal.

"I was going to tell you," she rushed to assure him, "but I was afraid you'd force me to quit my job and I wasn't ready…" She cut herself off, dismayed by how petty she sounded.

"You weren't ready." Out of the corner of her eye, she could see his hands gripping the edge of the chair he sat in, as he fought to rein in his incredulity. "Is that all you ever think of—yourself? What about the baby?" he demanded with controlled rage. "What about *me?* I haven't slept or eaten or breathed in thirty-six hours because you didn't tell me what you were up to. If I had known you were interviewing Rawlings, I would have recognized his name and realized what you were up against, and I would have *protected* you. None of this would have happened!"

"I'm sorry," she whispered. Remorse twisted through her, wringing tears from her heart. "I was going to tell you."

"Really?" he scoffed, his volume climbing. "After all the secrets you've kept from me, how do I know you had any intention of telling me at all?"

She gasped at the hurtful words, wrenching her gaze up in a desperate bid to convince him. "I was," she insisted. "On Christmas day, I was going to put the pregnancy strip in your... stocking." Her voice broke at the realization that that would never happen now. The poor little life inside of her had never stood a chance. She'd endangered it by continuing with her risky plan, knowing all the while how villainous a man Rawlings truly was. "Is he—did he get arrested yet for what he did to me?" she asked in a desperate bid to shift some of the blame off her own narrow shoulders.

"Not yet." Vinny sprang to his feet and stalked to the window, his agitation a clear sign that Rawlings' continued freedom chafed at him. "The cops and the district attorney want to make sure he won't find some kind of loophole to get around the charges."

An aching silence fell between them. Vinny kept his back to her. She watched his shoulders rise and fall as he fought to bring his emotions under control.

"I swear, Vinny," Ophelia said, in a last-ditch effort to elicit his understanding, "if I'd known what Rawlings would do to me, I would never have taken chances with our baby."

He turned his head at her assertion. But the look in his eyes wasn't even one that she recognized. He looked at her as if he'd never seen before—or like he was seeing for the first time who she really was. The look encased her heart in ice.

He had finally realized what she'd known all along—that she did not deserve him. That she wasn't the woman he thought she was.

"What else do you swear to?" he demanded, turning to face her, his hands curled into fists by his side. "That you never once considered aborting our baby? Is that why you didn't tell me you were pregnant?"

She longed to deny the accusation immediately, but the memory of considering abortion even for a fraction of a second kept her mute.

"I gotta get out of here," he declared, snatching his jacket off the back of the chair, "before I say something I'll regret." With fingers that shook, he jammed his arms through the sleeves as he walked to the door. Feeling lower than a worm crawling deep down in the earth, Ophelia could only watch him walk away.

As he reached for the latch, someone knocked.

With a scowl Vinny snatched the door open.

"Is she sleeping?" asked a familiar voice.

He held the door wordlessly ajar.

Stunned by the remote look on Vinny's face, Ophelia scarcely noticed her sister, Penny, peering around the door. With a dismissive look that made Ophelia's veins shrink, he slipped past Penny without another word.

"Hey." Penny divided a curious look between them as her son Ryan tugged her into the room. "Sorry it took so long for us to get here," she apologized. "Our flight was delayed." She sidled up to the bed, dismay registering on her pleasant face as she looked her sister over. "Oh, honey, you look awful." Blue-green eyes took stock of the cuts on Ophelia's face.

"I feel awful," Ophelia managed to whisper past the huge lump in her throat. Her gaze trekked to the little blond head standing at the height of her bed, near her elbow. Ryan peered up at her through rounded, worried eyes. "Hi, buddy," she crooned, sitting up straighter so as not to alarm him further, and willed herself not to cry in front of him. "Why don't you come sit up here?" She patted the space beside her hip, prompting Penny to lift him onto the mattress. "Fifi needs a hug," she added, using the name he'd bestowed on her.

As naturally compassionate as his mother, Ryan leaned into Ophelia, wrapped his sturdy little arms around her, and squeezed her hard. With her nose buried in his bright hair, it occurred to Ophelia that she would never get to cuddle her own baby like this. She'd failed to protect the little life the way she should have. Her face crumpled with misery.

"You hurt, Fifi?" Ryan asked, running a gentle hand over the bandage that encased her wrist as he peered up at her.

She tried once more to hide her tears from him and failed. "I'm hurt," she admitted in a voice thick with grief.

But it wasn't Rawlings whom she blamed; it was herself. She'd asked for every ounce of the misery filling her heart. She didn't deserve her loving husband. She didn't deserve a happy marriage. Not even the loss of her baby was punishment enough. It was about time she owned up to what a selfish, shallow creature she was. Time she showed some accountability for her actions. Just how she would accomplish such a feat, she didn't know, but it needed to be done. It was time to make some serious atonement.

VINNY SLANTED HIS wife a worried look. Seated next to him in the passenger seat of her reclaimed Kia Soul, she'd spoken scarcely more than a word since checking out of the hospital that morning. He'd brought her by his mama's house so she could say good-bye to his mother and sister, both of whom had been nearly as subdued as Lia. And now they were an hour outside of Philadelphia with hours to go before they reached Virginia Beach. He'd hoped putting distance between her and the man who'd nearly had her killed would bring some color back into her waxen cheeks, a little of that devil-may-care sparkle back to her lackluster eyes. But she remained silent and subdued, almost…penitent, if such a word could be used to describe her.

"You warm enough, *cara mia*?" The slate colored clouds were starting to dust I-95 with shimmering snowflakes. He had set the heat on high, but Lia still looked like she was freezing. She sat there hugging her injured arm like a bird with a broken wing, suppressing visible shudders. Was it the shock of having nearly been murdered or his harsh words that were eating at her?

"I'm fine." She stared unseeing at the road before them.

If Rawlings was the problem, maybe she only needed reassurance that he would be brought to justice—and soon. "I told you the latest update from Sergeant Presti, didn't I?" he asked, recalling that he had, but maybe she hadn't heard him.

"About the chauffeur?" she replied, proving as astute as ever. "Yeah, you told me."

Rawlings' driver, questioned by the police in relation to Lia's abduction and reappearance, had bolstered their case by rendering statements that implicated his employer. More than that, Lia's abductor, arrested for car theft, had stowed a Glock in his own car that was linked to the bullet that had killed John Staskiewicz. Finding himself facing murder charges, the kidnapper had fingered Collum as the man who'd hired him to abduct Lia. Phone calls between Collum and Rawlings, retrieved by the FBI, had sealed the lieutenant governor's fate. The man was being held without bond.

"Rawlings isn't going to get away with what he's done, if that's what's worrying you."

"It's not. Actually," she said, in a distant voice that did little to reassure him, "I could care less about Rawlings."

In that case, it had to be his behavior yesterday that had made her erect an invisible wall between them. "Look, I know we've got some stuff to talk about. Finding out that I was a father and I didn't even know it until the baby was gone—that was a mind fuck. I just don't understand why my wife—

my most trusted friend—would keep something like that from me. I'm sorry if I snapped, okay? I'm just a little on the defensive here."

To his astonishment, Lia socked him in the shoulder. "Don't do that!" she railed.

"Do what? What'd I do now?"

"You're apologizing! Why the hell are you apologizing when *I'm* the one who screwed up? I deserved every ounce of your anger and every harsh word you had to say to me."

"Baby, don't do this—"

"No, I have to. Right now I hate myself, and I've decided to move out for a while," she added.

What? The words were so unexpected that the steering wheel wobbled in his grip. "What do you mean 'move out'?" he asked, panic spiking his pulse.

"I just...I need some time alone, away from...us."

Us? He had to tear his horrified gaze off her profile to keep from crashing into the guardrail. Stabbing on the hazard lights, he swung her Kia off the highway and into the breakdown lane, where he turned in his seat to reason with her. "I don't understand. You gotta know I love you, no matter what."

"I know that." She turned her head to look at him. "But right now I don't love myself. I kept you in the dark when I shouldn't have. Because of my selfishness, I got our baby killed—"

"Lia."

"Let me talk. I don't deserve you, Vinny. I never have."

"Don't say that," he begged, his heart thudding with dread that she really meant what she was saying. "Of course you deserve me. That's bullshit." He tried groping for her hand, but she pulled it away and hugged herself harder.

"It's not bullshit. It's the truth." She turned her face away from him to stare into the trees beside the highway. "I'm going to move in with my sister for a while," she said dully.

"How can you say that?" Vinny demanded. "When Rawlings took you away from me, I couldn't even *breathe*, Lia. Don't you understand? I can't imagine my life without you. I don't even want to."

"You'll be better off," she insisted.

Taking in her stoic demeanor, he realized she was serious.

"Sweetheart, we can work this out," he told her. "We've always worked things out."

Her solemn expression offered him no hope. "Not this time," she said simply.

Shocked into silence, Vinny turned his attention to the cars tearing past them. They had four more hours on the road before they got home. Something told him that four hours wouldn't be enough time in which to change Lia's mind—probably not even four days or even a week. They'd come upon a huge, unforeseeable knot in their bond as husband and wife, one that made him quail for how convoluted and complicated it appeared.

Being a SEAL, his first impulse was to tackle the problem head-on, to unravel the knot, and smooth things out between them. But his gut whispered that this problem wasn't something he could fix. Only Lia, given time to heal and the space to remember how much they meant to each other, could untangle the knot from her end. All he could do was relinquish her in the hopes that she would realize they were better together than apart.

With his heart sinking like a stone, he merged back into traffic resigned to the fact that, for an unknown length of time, he was going to have to go through life without Lia right beside him.

CHAPTER EIGHT

"DAT'S A LICORICE card," Ryan stated, pointing a pudgy finger at the spot where Ophelia's gingerbread man was about to land. "You have to skip a turn."

"Are you sure?" Ophelia reached for the licorice card and turned it over. "Huh, you have the cards memorized," she marveled.

He had trounced her at a memory game earlier that day, and she didn't even know how he played those games on his Nintendo DS. At only three years of age, Ryan's situational awareness reminded her of Vinny. "I bet you have a photographic memory, too," she wagered, realizing now why she constantly lost to a three year old. "You're cheating," she added under her breath.

Ryan looked up sharply from the board that lay on the living room floor between them. "I not cheatin'!" he said, his little eyes ablaze with indignation.

"No, of course not," she soothed, cursing her quick tongue. "That's not what I meant, honey. It's just that your eyes take pictures and your head stores them, so you never forget anything you see."

Duh. The look on Ryan's face conveyed plainly that this was obvious. He probably thought it was the same for everyone. Ophelia snorted at his expression. Nothing amused her more than the looks on Ryan's face. They made her wonder if her own baby would have been so amusing, so precocious, so damn *smart*. Of course he—or she—would have. Any child of Vinny's was bound to be a prodigy.

For the fifth time that day, she caught herself reaching for her cell phone. *Don't call him.* She was the one who'd insisted that they live apart. She'd refused to be the thorn in his side, the weak link in their marriage, any longer. She had walked out of their life together because he was better off without her. Calling and talking to him like they were friends would be counter-productive.

Except that she missed him so much that she physically ached for him. She dreamed about him every night. She ate like a bird, with little appetite to speak of and had timed how frequently she thought about him—every three minutes, or less. All that had been going on for four weeks now.

She wanted so badly to tell him about the steps she was taking to improve herself. Even with her wrist still healing, she went to fitness classes three times a week and to church with Penny and Joe every Sunday. She had volunteered with Penny at the homeless shelter for veterans. She'd cut back on her hours at work in order to look after Ryan so Penny could save on daycare. It was the least she could do since Penny and Joe had taken her in on a moment's notice. Best of all, she'd discovered that she wasn't such an awful role model, after all. Even Joe had said she had a special way with little kids— though come to think of it, that might have been Joe's idea of a joke about Vinny's age and relative height.

No, she *was* good with Ryan. If she weren't, he wouldn't want to hang out with her all the time. She would make a good mother, after all. And she was dying to tell Vinny about her epiphany.

Except that Vinny hadn't called. And Ophelia had her pride. She rolled over onto her back, stared up at the family room ceiling, and sighed. *What if he's waiting for me to call him?*

"I winned," Ryan stated, matter-of-factly.

"Of course you did."

His piquant face loomed over hers. "Is I good today?" he demanded.

Being good was high on his list of objectives since Santa Claus would know if he wasn't, and Santa was due to bring toys in just two days. "You were an angel," Ophelia declared.

He frowned his disgust. "I wanna be a dinosaur."

"Well, then you'd have to be a dinosaur that doesn't eat other dinosaurs."

"Like a stegosaurus." He leapt to his feet, grabbed the book on dinosaurs off the coffee table, and plopped down with it.

Seeing Ryan engrossed in the book, Ophelia teased the phone out of her pocket and stared at the empty display. She could call Vinny and leave a friendly message. That way he wouldn't just forget about her. What if he never thought about her the way she thought of him? What if he found some-body else!

She'd dialed his number before she realized what she'd done. *Just to hear his voice*, she told herself. He was probably at work anyway, so she'd just end up getting his voice mail.

"Lia." The sound of her name being said with so much warmth and welcome brought a lump to her throat. "How you doin', *cara mia*?"

The endearment made her eyes sting. "Good. Great, in fact. Really good. You?"

"Oh...I've been better."

The sorrow in his voice strummed her heartstrings. "Why, what's wrong?"

A bitter chuckle sounded in her ear. "Nothin' now, *cara mia.*"

Relief buoyed her heart. Did her call mean that much to him? God, she hoped so. "I've missed you," she admitted, aware that Ryan had pulled his head out of the book and was now looking at her.

"I've missed you more," Vinny said, causing her heart to leap with joy. So he hadn't forgotten about her. "How's the wrist?"

"All better. Are you at work?" she asked.

"At the commissary. I'm lookin' for something to take to the XO's Christmas party—you know, the one he has every year?"

"Of course." Her heart clutched at the memory of past parties and the fun they'd had together.

"I thought I'd get some crackers and cheese. Maybe veggies and hummus."

"I thought you didn't like hummus."

"I like anything you like."

She seized his olive branch with a rush of gratitude. "Well, I like dressing up and going out," she hinted heavily. "I haven't gone out in forever."

"Then why don't I pick you up at eighteen hundred hours tomorrow, and we'll go to the party together?"

She would prefer to go anywhere else in the world than to a party where his teammates were bound to regard her with contempt. Still, beggars could not be choosers. "Okay," she agreed.

"See you tomorrow then. Bye."

The phone clicked in her ear making her wonder if Vinny was as eager to get together as she'd initially perceived. Perhaps she'd projected her desire onto him? Either way, the dark cloud that had been hanging over her head just minutes earlier had disappeared. Suddenly, the future looked worth living.

VINNY FROWNED AT his reflection in the bathroom mirror as he wrestled with his necktie. The gaunt, narrow face of the man looking back at him testified to how miserable he'd been without Lia in his life. Not feeling like he had the right to call her, not hearing the sound of her voice for weeks on end had nearly killed him. Sure, he'd been away from her plenty of times before for work, but he'd always managed to do sporadic video conferencing and the occasional phone call. The knowledge that she was waiting for him had made separation bearable.

Remembering her phone call yesterday, he marveled at his restraint. He'd wanted to sob with relief that she'd finally called him. Instead, he'd held it together long enough to secure a date with her the next night and then he'd quickly hung up before his emotions betrayed him. His patience had finally paid off! Christ, giving her the space to grieve their baby and to realize how much their marriage meant to her had been the hardest thing he'd ever done in his life. And Vinny had faced some enormous challenges.

I've got her now, though, he assured his harried reflection. "Fucking tie." He tugged it apart and started over.

Tonight was the turning point in their present situation. Nervousness fizzed in his belly. He hoped to God he'd gotten the details right, or she might yet slip from his grasp again. To bolster his confidence, he considered the news he had to share with her, confident that it would help to bring her home. She'd soon be back in his life, back in his bed, right where she belonged.

"WON'T WE BE late for the party?" Ophelia asked as Vinny pointed his Civic away from the beachfront toward Norfolk.

"Nah, they're starting later this year. I wanted to take you somewhere else first." His dark gaze trekked in her direction, lingering with appreciation on her figure-hugging, fire-engine red velvet dress.

She was glad now that she'd dressed to kill. *Looking like a million bucks*, as her sister said, gave her the confidence she needed to portray herself as the changed woman that she was, a woman worthy of her husband.

For his part, Vinny didn't seem to have too much to say. She studied him surreptitiously as they screamed down Highway 264. Looking debonair in his black suit and bright red Christmas tie, it was nonetheless apparent that he'd lost some weight. Did that mean he'd been as miserable as she'd been?

Ten minutes later, he drove his car onto a ramp exiting toward the Norfolk Waterfront. "Just where are you taking me?" she inquired, her curiosity growing.

"Can't tell you. It's a surprise."

Anticipation bubbled in her breast. "Something tells me we're not going to the XO's party," she wagered, admiring the pretty Christmas lights twinkling on the boardwalk. Even on Christmas Eve, Town Point Park and Waterside Mall attracted a healthy crowd of visitors.

"What makes you say that?" He swung into a parking lot near the marina and killed the engine. "I thought we'd just take a walk first."

He popped out of the car and was opening her door before she could question him further. "Button up," he said, taking it upon himself to fasten the top two buttons of her coat. The brush of his knuckles against her chin made her heart melt. Penny and Joe tolerated her company, but only Vinny ever coddled her. When he reached for her hand, it was all she could do not to hang onto him like a teenager in her first crush.

He drew her past a row of brightly lit specialty boutiques and a restaurant emitting a delicious aroma, but he didn't slow his pace until they neared the marina where sailboats rocked gently at their moorings. Their masts, strung with festive Christmas lights, swayed back and forth. The *Spirit of Norfolk* cruise ship gleamed like a porcelain gravy dish floating on the dark river. "Let's go on board," Vinny suggested, stepping up to the ticket kiosk.

Ophelia pulled back and looked at him. "We're going on board?" She's suspected Vinny of having a plan up his sleeve, but a Christmas Eve cruise in lieu of the usual SEAL team party surpassed her wildest expectations.

"I hope you don't mind. I took the liberty of making reservations. DeInnocentis, party of two," he told the booth attendee, who handed him their tickets.

"Oh, Vinny." The last time they'd taken this particular cruise together, he had proposed to her, going down on one knee in front of guests and crew. That had been the best night of her life. "You shouldn't have," she pretended to scold while inwardly celebrating.

"Well, it's too late to cancel now," he reasoned, hustling her up the gang plank to the first deck.

The night of his proposal, they had sat with a large group of people unknown to them. Tonight, the hostess led them to a table for two, right next to the window. Vinny pulled her chair out and Ophelia sank into it, her heart clutching at the sight of a rose bouquet and a bottle of champagne. Tears of gratitude stung her eyes. After all she'd done to sabotage their marriage, he still wanted her back.

The hostess expertly opened the bottle and poured them each a glass of chilled, bubbly liquid, wished them a romantic evening, and walked away. Ophelia peeked outside, watching the crew free the cruise ship from its moorings. In the next instant, a whistle sounded and the ship powered into the moonlit river.

She sat back in her chair and looked at him. She might have been the catalyst behind Jay Rawlings' indictment on kidnapping and murder charges and his immediate removal from the list of vice presidential candidates, but she had put her husband through hell and nearly destroyed everything precious to both of them in the process.

With her eyes, she sought to convey how sorry she was for putting him through the wringer. Holding her eyes, he sent her a pained smile.

The waitress laid an appetizer of shrimp cocktail before them, but it remained untouched as they nursed their champagne. Vinny struck her as oddly quiet—nervous, almost.

"The guys on the team made you somethin' for Christmas," he suddenly recollected. Pulling his cell phone from his jacket, he accessed an app and handed it across the table to her. "It's a video," he explained at her puzzlement. "Hit play."

Bemused, Lia tapped the triangle, and the video began. A scene opened onto four of Vinny's teammates sitting around a bonfire—Chief Harlan and three more men. The camera zeroed in on Harley, whose bright blue eyes reflected the firelight. "So, Lia," he said, addressing her directly, "we're having this pow-pow because we want you to know how much you mean to us and to Vinny. It's true that we don't always see eye to eye. You get him into trouble now and then and you take him away from us when we want to hang out."

Haiku, a Japanese-American SEAL leaned in. "And I'll never forgive you for spilling your beer on my pool table."

"Right. But we want you to know that we think you're pretty cool, otherwise," chimed in Teddy, the only African-American SEAL in Team Twelve. "And without you in his life, Vinny is pretty damn useless to us. He's a liability to the team and he's no fun to hang around with, anyway."

"Yeah, so we need you to forgive him for whatever he's done and come back to him," Haiku added.

"We're begging you, Lia," Chief Harlan pleaded. "And you know how hard it is for us to be humble. So, Merry Christmas, and here's to a better year next year with you and Vinny back together."

The cameraman gave a thumbs up, making Ophelia suspect that Vinny had been the one filming them. "You set that up," she accused.

"Nope, that was Senior Chief. The video was totally their idea."

His assertion brought a lump to her throat. She shook her head and heaved a sigh.

"What'sa matter, baby?" Vinny reached across the table and caught her hand. The warmth of his touch, his tenderness, made her want to throw herself onto his lap.

"You didn't tell them why I left," she pointed out. "They thought it was something *you* did."

He shrugged his shoulders. "It's none of their business."

Again, he'd covered for her. "I still don't deserve you," she realized, blinking back tears of frustration.

"Don't say that," he insisted, sounding suddenly agitated. "I need you in my life. I can't do this without you."

His heartfelt words encouraged her. "I've been working really hard to be a wife you can be proud of," she volunteered through a tight throat.

"I was already proud of you," he protested.

"As a person, I mean—not just a newswoman. I only work part time now. I've been babysitting Ryan every morning, and I'm *good* with him. I really am, Vinny."

"Of course you are. I never doubted that."

"I go to church now, and I exercise, and I even volunteered at a homeless shelter—"

"Sweetheart, you've got nothin' to prove to me," he insisted, squeezing her hand harder. "I've always loved you for who you are. I don't want you to change."

Tears of relief rushed into her eyes. "Thank you," she whispered.

"Just promise me something," he implored, his gaze delving deep into her eyes.

"Anything," she agreed, dashing away the tear that slipped between her lashes.

"Promise me you won't keep any secrets from me, ever again. There isn't anything in the world that we can't face together. I want to be able to *protect* you next time."

"I promise," she told him, nodding her understanding. He'd wanted to protect her and she hadn't let him.

"So, you'll come home with me tonight?" he asked with a pleading look that she had never been able to resist.

She felt herself grinning for the first time in weeks. The thought of sleeping in Vinny's arms on their California king instead of Penny's firm guest bed filled her with a heady longing to be there right now. She almost wished the cruise ship would turn around now, taking them back to the harbor so they could get home all the sooner.

"I want to come home," she agreed, threading her fingers through his. "I've missed us so much."

"I've missed us, too," he said gruffly.

The waitress reappeared just then, bearing their main course. With Vinny distracted, Ophelia toed off one of her high-heeled shoes and slid a stocking-clad foot up the inside of his leg. Watching him fight to keep his composure as he shook out his napkin and reached for his fork made her ribs ache with contained laughter.

"Is this my Christmas gift?" he inquired after the waitress moved away. The glint in his dark eyes warned her that she was asking for trouble.

"M-hmm," she confirmed, caressing his powerful inner thighs with her dexterous toes.

"I got a surprise for you, too." He carved a bite out of his steak and chewed it carnivorously. "But it's not what you think," he added, intriguing her with that bit of information.

"It's not?"

"It's news," he added waggling his black eyebrows, "that you'll have to extort from me before the night is over."

"Oh, I'm good at extorting information," she purred as she stroked his thigh.

"I know you are, baby. Eat your food." He gestured to her plate with his fork.

She took an obliging bite of steak and found it tender enough to melt in her mouth. When was the last time she had felt like eating? "Mmm, so, about this news," she began, turning over thoughts in her head. "Might it have anything to do with your application to medical school?" She'd been dying to hear the verdict since he'd first applied for early consideration.

"God, you're good." He shook his head.

Her fork clattered from her hand onto her plate. "You got accepted?" she cried in delight. "To where? Which one?"

"MCV in Richmond." It had been his first choice.

She had to clap a hand to her mouth to stifle a scream.

"There's a caveat," he warned her. "We'll have to move this summer." He sent her a searching look. "Which means you'll have to quit your job and find a new one."

Her momentary panic came and went. "No worries. Corruption exists in every city. I'm sure I can find a new job."

"I'm sure you can, too," he stated.

She considered the news as she chewed thoughtfully. Her career was not the only one that would change. "So this is it," she marveled. "You're actually going to leave the Teams." She searched his expression for signs of regret.

"It's time," he said with certainty. Having enlisted at the tender age of 17, his two four-year terms had made a man out of him, guiding his decision to become a medical doctor.

The realization that she wouldn't have to fear for his life, day in and day out, filled her with bottomless relief. Their future together had never looked brighter. If only they weren't stranded on a boat now headed past the Norfolk Naval Base. Turning her head, she sought the stairs that gave access to the other levels.

"Oh, I know what you're thinking," Vinny drawled. "I don't think we could get that lucky twice."

They'd found an empty pantry on their last cruise and made the best possible use of it.

"Besides," he continued, pitching his voice lower, "tonight, I plan to take my time." He leered. "I haven't had you to myself in weeks."

She arched a skeptical eyebrow. "Since when have you ever taken your time?" she quipped.

"Do I hear you complaining?"

"Nope."

"Didn't think so."

The only thing in the world Ophelia could possibly have complained about at that moment was the speed at which their ship was moving. She could not wait to get home to their condo on Shore Drive to continue the life they'd started together five years ago.

EPILOGUE

"HAPPY VALENTINE'S DAY, sweetheart." Ophelia greeted Vinny at the door in a red lace teddy, matching garters, black stockings, and five-inch heels.

"Jesus, God," he exclaimed, running a stunned gaze down and up her body and shutting the door hastily behind him, lest every man on Shore Drive get a peek. "Sorry I'm late." He thrust a bouquet of long-stemmed roses at her. "I had to run over an old man and steal these from him 'cause the store was all sold out," he asserted.

She clucked her tongue. "Poor old man." Accepting the bouquet, she took a long dreamy sniff. "They're lovely, thank you. How was work?" she inquired, as he shrugged out of his winter BDU jacket.

"Busy," he said tiredly. But suddenly, seeing her like this, he didn't feel tired at all, even though he'd been on the job since five. He reached for his wife, unwilling to talk about work, when the smell of something burning hit the back of his throat. "What's that smell?"

"Dinner," she said with a shrug. But for once, instead of it seeming to bother her, she swiveled on her bare feet and sashayed ahead of him into their kitchen.

He realized with a rush of tenderness that, as always, she'd done her best to make the evening perfect. So what if she couldn't cook. "Smells great," he lied.

"The scallops didn't come out the way I expected." Running the rose stems under the faucet, she reached for scissors.

He stepped up behind her, searching for supportive words. "That's okay. It's the effort that counts. You'll get the hang of it."

"Doubtful," she replied, snipping an inch off the stems and sticking the roses in the vase that sat on the windowsill.

Vinny put his hands on her bare shoulders and turned her around to face him. "And if you don't ever get it right, then we'll eat takeout every night," he persisted. "As long as we're together, I don't care."

Her gaze trekked to the table where he saw that she'd set it with their best china, a bottle of wine, and a lacey tablecloth. "I wanted to make it perfect," she admitted.

"It *is* perfect."

"Well, the salad turned out okay," she said a little more brightly.

"I'm on a diet anyway." He slid another appreciative gaze over her lingerie-clad body. "You want to eat now or later?"

"Later," she said with a slow smile. "Right now I have a present to give you."

Figuring he knew what kind of present she had in mind, Vinny scooped her up, ignoring her shriek of protest and carried her into the living room, where the drapes were drawn. A gas fire flickered warmly in the fireplace. She'd draped a fur throw over their L-shaped couch.

"Nice," he commented, depositing her gently on top of it. His lips, like a heat seeking missile, closed unerringly over hers.

"Mmm. Wait," she said against his mouth. One hand pushed against his shoulder, urging him off her. The other sank into his short, crisp hair, pulling him back for another sultry kiss.

"What do you want?" he asked, confused by her mixed signals.

"I mean I really have a gift to give you first. It's right there on the end table."

Peering over the arm of the couch, Vinny spied what looked like a box of chocolates wrapped in red cellophane and topped with a white bow. "You want me to open it now?" The dusky suggestion of her nipples peeking up at him proved distracting. "I'd rather unwrap you first," he declared, lowering his head to lap at the firm nubs through the gauzy fabric.

"Later then," she decided breathlessly.

At her encouragement, he slipped to his knees beside the couch and proceeded to divest her of her enticing garment, inch by tantalizing inch.

Many minutes later, Vinny collapsed along the length of the couch, pulled her into his arms, and flipped the throw over their naked bodies. He kissed her forehead. "God, I love our life together," he mumbled.

She smiled like a cat that had eaten the canary. "I'm glad you said that." She lifted her head off his shoulder and reached for the gift he'd left for later. "Open it now."

What he'd thought was a box of chocolates proved too light. Bemused, Vinny tugged off the bow, lifted the lid, and peeked inside. A white plastic test strip with an unmistakable plus sign looked out at him from a bed of velvet. First surprise, then astonishment, then euphoria broke over him in successive waves, rendering him speechless.

"I'm six weeks pregnant," Lia announced, her eyes dancing with joy. "Looks like we had our own Christmas miracle."

"Holy shit." Vinny had never doubted his ability to get Lia pregnant; he'd accomplished everything he'd ever set his sights on. He just hadn't expected it to happen so soon.

"You'll just be starting med school, and I'll be working at a new job when the baby's born," she added, revealing a trace of her old self-doubt.

"Hey," he admonished. "Just love our baby the way you love me, and it'll all work out. There is nothing you and I can't handle together. Remember?"

"I remember," she said, brushing away happy tears.

After what had happened to her at Rawlings' hands, she would never forget it.

"I love you, Lia." He slid his arm beneath the throw and placed a large warm palm over her bare stomach, right over his child. "Thank you," he said, meaning it. "This is the best Valentine's Day present I could ever get."

"Just wait until the birth," she murmured, with a touch of wryness.

"That'll be a pretty damn great gift, too."

DANGER CLOSE

BOOK #1 ECHO PLATOON SERIES

LATE SPRING 2014

Marliss Melton

JAMES-YORK PRESS

PROLOGUE

The Mark V-1 Special Operations Craft slid with a hiss onto a deserted strip of moonlit shore. Lurching to a stop, it delivered a four-man fire team of Navy SEALs at their insertion point on the Mexican side of the Rio Grande River. Lt. Sam Sasseville stripped off his night ops jacket, stuffing it into the gunwale locker, before giving his teammates the go-signal and leaping ashore with a lightweight pack. His three teammates followed his lead, their footfalls swift and stealthy, even with the added weight they carried and the mud sucking at their boots.

Beneath the jackets they'd discarded, they had dressed to resemble civilians. Wearing dark cargo pants with pockets full of extra ammo and baggy black T-shirts to conceal an arsenal of weapons, they melted into the darkness. A Gerber blade splinted Sam's left ankle. His backpack, like every other man's, contained a helmet with NVGs attached, several Meals-Ready-to-Eat, baby wipes for keeping clean, and a fresh T-shirt. Sam's pack also carried a satellite phone.

Sweeping jungle-green eyes over the flat, scrubby terrain, he assessed their location. A steady drizzle dampened waves of dark hair he'd inherited from his Cuban grandmother. A compliment of tan skin simplified his infiltration into the Mexican province of Tamaulipas.

Sam's three teammates didn't have it so easy. Bronco, Haiku, and Bullfrog had all slathered their bare skin in bronzing lotion. Bronco wore a floppy hat to cover his sun-streaked hair, while Bullfrog and Haiku, both brunettes, went hatless.

The lapping of water muffled the SEALs' trek across the mud flats to their predetermined location. As the K50S water jets on the Mark V-1 carried the craft silently back to the Gulf, the squad rallied, squatting amidst the marsh grass. They wouldn't need the delivery vehicle again. If everything went as planned, they would exfil via helo.

Sam checked his watch before shrugging off his pack and grubbing inside for his sat phone. A simple three-digit combination put him in touch with headquarters.

"Home plate," answered the ops officer, Lietenant Commander Lindstrom, who sat before a computer monitor at the Spec Ops Headquarters back in Dam Neck, Virginia.

"Heads up, Home plate," Sam replied, having fun with the baseball lingo they'd decided to use to encode their progress. "Tampa Bay Rays are at first base now, waiting for the ump to show up."

"Play ball, Rays," Lindstrom said with a snigger on his end.

"Here he comes now," Bronco stated, apparently spotting the "ump," through the high powered scope on his sniper rifle. "Right on time."

Over the patter of rain, Sam detected the purr of an approaching engine. Twin beams sheared the tops of the tall grass that hid them. The "ump" was a DEA officer who'd volunteered to help out. He would escort them into Matamoros, the lawless town situated across the U.S. border from Brownsville, Texas. There, the SEALs would initiate a twenty-four hour reconnaissance, monitoring the movements in and around the site, before sweeping in to recover their target. If all went well, they'd drive to the exfil site and fly off on a Navy Seahawk.

Easy Day. Sam simmered as he slipped the sat phone back into his pack. This whole goddamn op wouldn't be happening at all if Senator Lyle Scott's idiot daughter had left Matamoros when the U.S. embassy there issued the mandatory evacuation of all U.S. citizens. If not for her, Sam and his teammates would be headed for Malaysia as part of the effort to take out an infamous arms smuggler. Instead, he was playing nursemaid to a humanitarian aid worker who didn't have any sense of self-preservation. The silver spoon stuck in her mouth must have interfered with her deductive reasoning capabilities. He'd christened this mission "Operation Dumb Broad" in her honor.

"That's our guy," Bronco confirmed, lowering his weapon. The vehicle came to a squeaky stop and dimmed its lights.

"Go," Sam ordered.

Bullfrog darted out of hiding first, providing cover for Haiku and then Bronco, who leapfrogged his position. Sam brought up the rear and was the first into the rust-colored taxi, taking shotgun, as was his due as the officer in charge. His three companions squeezed into the back seat, grunting at the tight fit. Cigarette smoke filled the car's interior. The car boasted plastic-covered seats and a working meter.

The DEA officer tossed his Marlboro out the window and turned his head to glance at Sam. "Welcome to hell," he rasped, his eyes glinting in the dark. Engaging the meter like he meant to charge them by the kilometer, he hammered the accelerator, flinging them all back in their seats as the taxi took off.

Beyond the swinging crucifix that hung from the rearview mirrors and beyond the slapping windshield wipers, the glow of Matamoros beckoned them into danger.

Sam's resentment bubbled. The spitting sky, the time of year—late spring—and the circumstances of this op reminded him of an incident in high school, one that had formed his opinion of wealthy individuals, women especially. Back then, the source of his torment had been Wendy Fletcher—daughter of a real estate tycoon, prom queen, and the biggest tease in the twelfth grade. If he'd known the outcome of his heroics, he would have let her suffer the consequences of her flirtatiousness. Instead, her hoarse screams coming from the bedroom at an after prom party had awakened his protective instincts and sent him flying to her rescue.

Streetwise, with a private crush on Wendy Fletcher, Sam had thrashed her two male companions within an inch of their lives. He'd expected Wendy to at least thank him, but she hadn't. Those boys had been her friends, after all. And when her father demanded an explanation for her bruises, she had offered up Sam as a scapegoat.

He'd suffered a month in prison, his single mother too poor to pay bail or repay a bond, before his court appointed lawyer managed to prove his innocence. But even then, being Latino, from the wrong neighborhood, he'd been cast into the role of criminal, and no one would see past the stereotype, so he'd joined the Navy.

Since then, he had broken every stereotype into which he'd been cast, never quitting, until he'd become a warrior worthy of every man's respect—a US Navy SEAL.

Yet, here he was, as a Navy SEAL, putting himself and his teammates into peril for what?—to extricate the precious daughter of a wealthy politician who'd found herself in circumstances of her own making.

What the hell was she still doing here in Matamoros, when drug lords ruled the city? Or was she just too pampered, too naïve to realize what could happen to her in this lawless realm?

He supposed he was about to find out. Right now, the only certainty was that if he failed in this mission to extract Senator Lyle Scott's foolish daughter from this corrupted city, his career would be over—just like that. He could feel it in his bones. Everything he had fought so hard to accomplish could be stripped from him as if it had never happened. Why? Because Senator Scott played golf with the Commander in Chief himself.

As the lights of Matamoros brightened the water droplets on the windshield, Sam's stomach twisted with foreboding. The night he'd protected Wendy Fletcher and this one bore an eerie similarity, right down to the time of year and the weather. No wonder he suffered a premonition that history was about to repeat itself.

Rave Reviews for
MARLISS MELTON

THE ENFORCER

"If a reader is looking for grass-roots realism, that's what they'll find in this well-written tale, steeped in the hardships of those who have experienced the horrors of war. THE ENFORCER is in a league of its own."

—InD'tale Magazine

THE GUARDIAN

"Well, Marliss Melton does it again. Packs a book full of action, suspense, mystery and romance."

—Lorelei's Lit Lair

THE PROTECTOR

"...the kind of intrigue I enjoy, much like Tom Clancy, Vince Flynn, David Baldacci, and Steig Larsen. In my opinion they have nothing on her."

—Lt. Col. John Lund, U.S. Air Force, ret.

SHOW NO FEAR

"If you enjoy good suspense, lots of action, plenty of plot twists and realistic romance, then Marliss Melton's *Show No Fear* is for you."

—Novel Reviews, Book Reviews

TOO FAR GONE

"Likeable and honorable characters who elicit sympathy and/or empathy…"

—RomRevToday.com

DON'T LET GO

"4 Stars! Another winner in a top-notch series! …"

—Romantic Times BOOKreviews Magazine

NEXT TO DIE

"Melton brings her considerable knowledge about the military and intelligence world to this Navy SEAL series."

—Freshfiction.com

TIME TO RUN

"Melton...doesn't miss a beat in this involving story."

—Publishers Weekly

IN THE DARK

"Hooked me from the first page..."

—Lisa Jackson, *NYT Bestselling Author*

FORGET ME NOT

"A wonderful book, touching all the right heartstrings. I highly recommend it!"

—Heather Graham, *NYT Bestselling Author*

Novels by
MARLISS MELTON

THE TASKFORCE SERIES

THE PROTECTOR (Aug 2011)

THE GUARDIAN (Feb 2013)

THE ENFORCER (Sept 2013)

TEAM TWELVE NAVY SEALS SERIES

FORGET ME NOT (Dec 2004)

IN THE DARK (June 2005)

TIME TO RUN (Feb 2006)

NEXT TO DIE (August 2007)

DON'T LET GO (April 2008)

TOO FAR GONE (Nov 2008)

SHOW NO FEAR (Sept 2009)

LONG GONE, A Novella (Nov 2012)

Author Bio

Marliss Melton is the author of over thirteen novels featuring warriors of the present and the past. In writing her Navy SEAL Team Twelve series and her Taskforce trilogy, Marliss relied on her experience as a military spouse and on her many contacts in the Spec Ops and Intelligence communities with the goal of penning realistic and heartfelt stories about America's most elite warriors and fearless agency heroes. Daughter of a U.S. foreign officer, Melton grew up in various countries overseas. She has taught English, Spanish, ESL, and Linguistics at the College of William and Mary, her alma mater. Teaching History of the English Language informed her research of medieval England for her Medieval Warriors series. She lives in Williamsburg, Virginia, with her husband and daughter, the youngest of their six children still at home. Be sure to "friend" Marliss on Facebook! Visit www.marlissmelton.com for more information.

Made in the USA
Columbia, SC
27 February 2023

13025799R00080